LONE STAR CHRISTMAS

BY
CATHY GILLEN THACKER

MILLS & BOON

Published in Great Britain 2014
by Mills & Boon, an imprint of Harlequin (UK) Limited,
Eton House, 18-24 Paradise Road, Richmond, Surrey, TW9 1SR

© 2014 Cathy Gillen Thacker

ISBN: 978-0-263-91343-9

23-1214

Harlequin (UK) Limited's policy is to use papers that are natural, renewable and recyclable products and made from wood grown in sustainable forests. The logging and manufacturing processes conform to the legal environmental regulations of the country of origin.

Printed and bound in Spain
by CPI, Barcelona

"How did that get in my pocket?"

Nash flashed a sexy grin as he held a sprig of mistletoe above Callie's head. UB

He knew he wasn't playing fair, using their attraction for each other to draw Callie all the way into the present. But there were times, like now, when it was the best way to make her see that the past was over. There was no use hiding behind it, not when they had a connection as fierce as the chemistry between them. Hooking the toe of his boot beneath the rung of a chair, he brought it all the way from the table and sank into it, dropping the mistletoe and pulling her onto his lap on the process. "Nash…"

He drew back to see into her eyes, knowing he didn't need a cornball excuse to kiss her, touch her, hold her. "Kiss me, Callie…"

Wreathing her arms around his neck, she turned her head to his and smiled with a devastating mix of tenderness and mischief. "Is that your Christmas wish?"

He grinned. "One of them."

Cathy Gillen Thacker is married and a mother of three. She and her husband spent eighteen years in Texas and now reside in North Carolina. Her mysteries, romantic comedies and heartwarming family stories have made numerous appearances on bestseller lists, but her best reward, she says, is knowing one of her books made someone's day a little brighter. A popular Mills & Boon® author for many years, she loves telling passionate stories with happy endings, and thinks nothing beats a good romance and a hot cup of tea! You can visit Cathy's website, www.cathygillenthacker.com, for more information on her upcoming and previously published books, recipes and a list of her favorite things.

Chapter One

Nash Echols dropped a fresh-cut Christmas tree onto the bed of a flatbed truck. Watched, as a luxuriously outfitted red SUV tore through the late November gloom and slammed to an abrupt stop on the old logging trail.

"Well, here comes trouble," he murmured, when the driver door opened and two equally fancy peacock-blue boots hit the running board, then the ground.

His glance moved upward, taking in every elegant inch of the cowgirl marching toward him. He guessed the sassy spitfire to be in her early thirties, like him. She glared while she moved, her hands clapped over her ears to shut out the concurrent whine of a dozen power saws.

Nash lifted a leather-gloved hand.

One by one his crew stopped, until the Texas mountainside was eerily quiet, and only the smell of fresh-cut pine hung in the air. And still the determined woman advanced, chin-length dark brown curls framing her even lovelier face.

He eased off his hard hat and ear protectors.

Indignant color highlighting her delicately sculpted cheeks, she stopped just short of him and propped her hands on her slender denim-clad hips. "You're killing me, using all those chain saws at once!" Her aqua-blue eyes narrowed. "You know that, don't you?"

Actually, Nash hadn't. And given the fact his crew had only been at this a few hours…

Her chin lifted another notch. "*You have to stop!*"

At that, he couldn't help but laugh. It was one thing for this little lady to pay him an unannounced visit, another for her to try to shut him down. "Says who?" he challenged right back.

She angled her thumb at her sternum, unwittingly drawing his glance to her full, luscious breasts beneath the fitted red velvet western shirt, visible beneath her open wool coat. "Says me!"

He took in the hefty diamond engagement and wedding rings glinting on her left hand, squinted and asked in a way he knew would rankle, "Just out of curiosity, ma'am, does your *husband* know what you're up to?"

For a moment, his uninvited visitor seemed caught off guard. Perplexed, almost. Then she stiffened and squared her shoulders, even more militantly. "For your information, cowboy, I don't need 'permission' from anyone."

Amused, he looked her over slowly, head to toe. "Then your husband wouldn't *mind* you creating a ruckus?"

Another long, thoughtful pause. Followed by a glimmer of inscrutable emotion in her eyes. "No," she said finally. And without another word, left it at that.

Which meant what? he wondered. Her husband was used to her temperamental ways? Or was just so weak he had no say? Her cagey expression gave no clue. Nash knew one thing, however. If she were *his* woman he wouldn't want her out here, stirring up trouble with a group of cattle and horse wranglers temporarily turned lumberjacks. "And you are?"

"Callie McCabe-Grimes."

Of course she was from one of the most famous and powerful clans in the Lone Star State. He should have figured that out from the moment she'd barged onto his property.

Nash indicated the stacks of freshly cut Christmas trees around them, aware the last thing he needed in his life was another person not into celebrating the holidays. "Sure that's not Grinch?"

Her thick lashes narrowed. "Ha, ha." She blew out a frustrated breath. "I'm your neighbor, to the east."

Ah, yes. Nash nodded. "The owner of the Heart of Texas Ranch and Corporate Retreat."

He'd heard that the hot-shot marketing wiz had apparently decided to stop helping everyone else get rich and go into business for herself. And while Nash respected the latter, he detested dealing with the diva-offspring of famous Texas families. Especially those who felt that, by virtue of their name and connections, they should automatically rule whatever roost they found themselves inhabiting.

"Well, then," Callie huffed, "if you know that, then you also know that my business is located in the valley between Sanders Mountain and Echols Mountain."

Lifting a brow, Nash took in the pink color staining her pretty face and the mutinous twist of her soft, voluptuous lips. "So?"

"So—" she waved at the dozen chain saw-wielding cowboys behind him, and the other six wrapping up recently shorn holiday trees "—all that racket you are making is carrying over onto my property!"

Nash squinted at the searing emotion in her eyes. This conversation was getting stranger all the time. "What did you expect when you set up shop next to a lumber operation?"

"There was no lumber operation when I purchased the property six months ago!"

Nash supposed that was true enough. He shrugged. "Well, there is now."

Panic warred with the fury on her face. "Since when?"

"Since I inherited the property from my great-great-uncle two months ago."

Callie sobered. "I'm sorry to hear about Mr. Echols's passing."

Nash studied her, pushing aside his own lingering grief. "You knew my uncle Ralph?"

"No," she admitted kindly. "I never had the pleasure."

"But if he was anything like me…?" Nash couldn't resist goading.

The stubborn look was back. Callie folded her arms in front of her in a way that delectably plumped up her breasts. "Let's hope he wasn't."

Nash tore his gaze from the inviting softness. Unable to resist teasing her a little more, however, he grinned. "Hasn't anyone ever told you it's the season to be jolly?"

Callie sighed in exasperation and shoved her hands through her chocolate-brown curls. "First of all, cowboy, it's not even Thanksgiving yet."

Yet, for him and his business, anyway, time was a wastin'. "It will be three days from now."

Callie threw up her palms in frustration. "Three days in which I will *lose my mind* if this racket keeps up."

No doubt about that. After all, from what he'd witnessed thus far, she did seem a little high-strung. He shifted his gaze to the pouting ripeness of her lips. Damned if he wasn't longing to kiss her, here and now, even though he knew as a married woman she was strictly off-limits.

Slowly, he let out a breath and returned his thoughts to the murky business at hand.

"And what would you have me do about it?" he asked grimly.

"I don't know." She paused to bite her lip, then asked, "Use one chain saw at a time?"

This time, Nash wasn't the only one who laughed.

When the ruckus from the men standing behind him quieted down, he winked at her and said glibly, "I'll think about it."

She stamped closer, not stopping until she was just inches away from him. "I want you to do a lot more than think about it, cowpoke!"

Nash took exception to her tone.

Her attitude.

Hell, just about everything about her.

His own temper rising, he schooled her quietly. "My name is Nash. Or Mr. Echols to you. And if that's all…"

Before he even had one ear covered up again, she planted her hand in the middle of his chest. Warmth spread instantly from beneath her delicate palm. Pooling in his chest, sliding ever downward, past his waist, to the place he least wanted to feel a rising pulse.

"Hold on there a minute, cowboy!" she declared. "I'm not done!"

Heart pounding, Nash plucked her hand from his chest like some odious piece of trash. "Too bad, little lady. Because I am."

She sniffed indignantly. "You can't just start up something like this without considering how it's going to affect everyone around you!"

Nash smiled. "Seems like—in your view anyway—I already have." He put the sound guards back on his head, then the hard hat, and gave his men the signal to resume.

She propped both hands on her hips. And this time she did stomp her pretty little foot as the whine of power saws echoed in the cool late November air.

Nash couldn't hear her muffled words of outrage, but he sure could see Callie McCabe-Grimes mouthing *something* as she glared at him, slapped her palms over her ears and spun on her heel. Her hips swaying provocatively, long luscious legs eating up the ground, she marched back to her truck and climbed into the cab. Then she extended her arm out the window, looked him right in the eye and offered him a surprisingly unladylike gesture before turning her pickup around and peeling away.

He stood there a moment, chuckling at her moxie. It was a good thing their personalities mixed about as well as oil and water, he thought, watching the dust fly in her wake. Otherwise a woman that beautiful and spirited could easily waylay him. And a distraction like that was something he did not need.

Especially at this time of year.

"THERE MUST BE *something* I can do to stop that big buffoon!" Callie complained to her sister Lily over Skype, as soon as she got back to the ranch.

With the cool expertise of an accomplished attorney, Lily McCabe rocked back in her desk chair, at her Laramie, Texas, law office, and listened intently.

Doing her best to calm her racing pulse, Callie persisted. "Nash Echols has got to be violating some noise regulation—or something with all that racket!"

Lily shook her head. "First of all, there are no noise ordinances in rural areas."

Callie bit down on an oath. It was bad enough that her next-door neighbor was incredibly annoying, but at six foot two, with a lumberjack's powerful build, shaggy wavy black hair and slate-gray eyes, he was also handsome enough to grace an outdoor-living magazine cover. Not that his rugged good looks would help him where she was concerned...

"There are air rights," her sister continued practically. "But those belong to whoever is renting or residing on the property on which any noise is made. Which means any noise Nash Echols creates on his land is well within his rights."

Callie didn't care if Nash made himself deaf. It was her son—who luckily was still at nursery school—and the retreat clients set to start arriving the following week that she was worried about. Thankfully, though, at the moment she was the only one on her ranch, witnessing the ruckus.

"But his noise is coming over to my property! I mean, it's horrible." She opened up the window next to the phone, and just like before, the constant whine of multiple power saws reverberated in the brisk November air. She shut it again and turned back to the computer screen on her desk. "See what I mean?"

Lily nodded. "Just hearing it through the walls of your ranch house is enough to give me a headache—and I'm two hundred miles away! I can only imagine what it sounds like from your end."

"Exactly!"

Her sister picked up a pen and turned it end-over-end. "But you can't go to court on account of someone giving you a headache, Callie. Or the justice system would be jam-packed with nuisance cases."

Reluctantly, she supposed that was true.

Lily's demeanor gentled even more. "You want my honest advice, sis?"

Callie did her best to relax. Not easy, when she was still seeing—in her mind's eye, anyway—the smug expression on Nash Echols's blatantly handsome face. Still feeling the taut, warm muscles beneath the palm she had recklessly planted on his chest…

Callie swallowed, tamping down the whisper of long suppressed desire. She was romantically unattached now, and planned to stay that way.

"That is why I called you," she said quietly. Because, of all five of her sisters, Lily was always the quickest to cut to the chase with a solution.

"Go back. Apologize to the man. Tell him you temporarily lost your mind and want to work out an amicable solution, so that both your businesses can continue to operate."

The idea of groveling in front of the way-too-confident man next door rankled. Worse, just the thought of seeing him again made her pulse race.

Taking all that into account, Callie uttered a morose sigh and rubbed at the tense muscles in her forehead. "He's not going to go for it."

Frowning at her sister's defeatist attitude, Lily warned, "You better hope he does, because otherwise you're in a heap of trouble. In the holiday season, no less."

NASH HAD JUST gotten out of the shower when he heard a vehicle in the driveway. He pulled on a pair of jeans and, still rubbing a towel through his hair, walked barefoot to the front hall. The bell rang. Nash looped the towel around his neck, opened the heavy wood door and got his second surprise of the day.

On the other side of the portal was Callie McCabe-Grimes. She had a big wicker basket in one hand, and a handsome little toddler, clad in a tyke-size cowboy getup, in the other.

Although she was a married woman—with a kid, no less—and should be used to the sight of a partially disrobed man, she appeared taken aback by the sight of him. So much so that when she silently took in his bare chest and damp hair, she looked as if she wanted to bolt, but didn't.

Tightening her grip on the little boy's hand, and plastering a smile as big as Texas on her face, she said, "I'm here to apologize."

That *was* news.

Reluctantly, she lifted her eyes to his, and kept them there. "I'm afraid we got off on the wrong foot."

No joke.

"Hence, my son, Brian—" she indicated the curly-haired little boy beside her with a tilt of her head "—and I would like to make amends and start over."

If anyone had accompanied Callie for the mea culpa, Nash would have expected it to be her husband. But then, maybe Mr. Grimes didn't know what his little woman had been up to.

Nor did her son.

Unable to resist making things at least a little difficult for the Texas belle, Nash ran a hand across his jaw and pointed out, "*Brian* doesn't owe me an apology."

Callie flushed, obviously recalling her diva-like exit

from his property. "Yes, well, as I said…I forgot my manners momentarily. And I do feel terrible about that."

She felt terrible about something—that was clear. Exactly what that was, he wasn't entirely sure.

Still, he had been raised with manners, too, and since his new neighbor had taken what had to be a difficult first step toward reconciliation, he felt obligated to be cordial, as well.

He stepped aside, suddenly concerned about the drop in temperature. It was just above freezing now. "Would you like to come in? It's pretty cold outside for your little one."

"Yes, thank you. That would be nice." Ushering his guests inside and shutting the door behind them, he realized that the foyer was a little chilly compared to the warmth of the rest of the rustically outfitted log-cabin-style ranch house. But that didn't seem to bother Callie or her son.

She glanced around, taking in the soaring cathedral ceiling and large fieldstone fireplace in the adjacent living room. Her eyes fell on the leather furniture and earth-toned Southwestern rugs.

While his great-uncle Ralph had been alive, the Echols Mountain Ranch house had definitely been a man's domain. Nash hadn't changed much since he had arrived.

Nor did he intend to do so in the future.

Aware the domain seemed all the more masculine with someone as feminine as Callie in it, he asked casually, "How old is your son?"

"Two and a half."

Nash had never been one to gush over kids, but there was something about this little guy—maybe it was his resemblance to his mama?—that drew him in. He smiled, inclining his head at the tyke. "Cute."

"Thanks," Callie murmured. And this time her smile appeared genuine.

Looking ready to make himself at home, Brian took off his Stetson and attempted to fit it over the newel on the staircase. It fell to the floor instead. He reached for it, tried again and missed by an even wider margin.

Nash leaned down. "Let me help you, little fella."

"No," Brian retorted with the stubbornness he evidently got from his gorgeous, dark-haired mama. "*I* do."

Nash lifted his hands and stepped back.

Seeming torn between correcting her son and getting on with it, Callie blew out a breath and handed Nash the basket. "Inside you'll find our welcome-to-the-neighborhood dinner. Homemade Texas chili and cornbread, fruit compote and chocolate cake."

Nash couldn't recall the last time he'd had a hot, home-cooked meal. Most of his meals were either from a restaurant or the freezer section of the local supermarket.

"Seriously?"

She shrugged. "Nothing I wouldn't do for anyone else moving in."

Nash figured that was probably true.

"The chili and cornbread are still hot."

She was killing him; she had to know that.

Aware he was attracted when he shouldn't be, he went on a fishing expedition. "I imagine your husband is expecting you home soon?"

Again, that pause. A definite evasion.

"Ah, no," she said finally.

Which meant what? Nash wondered. Was she separated? Getting a divorce? Just unattended and unhappy?

Not that it was any of his business. Except, they were neighbors and, in the Lone Star State, anyway, neighbors looked out for one another.

Furthermore, his gut told him that Callie McCabe-Grimes definitely was in need of some—if not TLC—then, at least, amiable concern.

Meanwhile, little Brian was still tossing his hat at the newel post. And missing. Again. And again.

To her credit, Callie stood back and let the little fella keep on trying.

Aware he wouldn't mind a chance to ease the rift between them and get to know a little more about his new neighbors, Nash turned back to Callie. She was right—there was no time like the present to start over. "Have you and your son eaten?" he asked impulsively.

Callie blinked, clearly taken aback by the question. "Well, no…not yet…but…"

Nash gazed deep into her aqua-blue eyes and took another leap of faith. Maybe there was a helluva lot more to her than had first appeared. "Want to join me?"

Chapter Two

Nash Echols was a man who was full of surprises, Callie acknowledged. The least of which was his current chivalry. Which seemed, at the moment anyway, to be as deeply ingrained as her own usual good manners.

Had she confronted him about the ruckus in any other way, she might have had a very different result. But she hadn't, and now she had to deal with the consequences of her earlier outburst. And what was, at best, a very awkward situation.

Nash's sexy smile widened as he continued in a silky smooth voice that ratcheted up the tension inside her even more, "I'm more than willing to share this delicious spread. I assume you brought enough?"

Glad she had one of the most effective chaperones ever put on this earth with her, as well as a reason to depart quickly once her mission was accomplished, Callie nodded. "Except...Brian doesn't eat chili. It's too spicy."

His gray eyes twinkled. "Will he eat cornbread and fruit, and—" Nash paused, clearly thinking how to phrase it " —the last course?"

Callie nodded, aware her son was listening intently now—and clearly a little enamored of Nash. Maybe this was a good time to work out a solution to their mutual problem. "Oh, yes. He loves c-a-k-e."

"Cake, Mommy!" Brian yelled.

"Some things, he can spell," Callie said dryly.

Nash chuckled. "Well, then, we're all set."

Callie studied him cautiously, trying—and failing—not to be turned on by the sleek, suntanned skin over his wide, inviting shoulders and nicely sculpted chest and abs. "You're sure it's not an imposition?"

A slow grin tugged at the corners of his sensual lips. "I wouldn't have asked if it was. Dishes are in the cabinets. Help yourself. I'm going to finish getting dressed then I'll be right back."

Yes, dressed was a good idea.

Standing there talking with him, when he was only half-clothed, had conjured up a wellspring of longing that was destined to go unmet.

"Right back, Mommy," Brian echoed, snapping her out of her reverie.

Callie knelt to help her son off with his coat.

Nash headed upstairs. By the time he came back down, Callie had set out the food, situated Brian on a stack of phone books and pulled his chair up to the table.

Nash extended his hand. "Let's start over," he said, every bit the Texas gentleman now. "I'm Nash Echols."

Warmth spiraled through her. "Callie McCabe-Grimes," she added with a smile. "And my son, Brian."

Nash helped her with her chair. For the next few minutes, they talked about where they both grew up. Dallas for him, Laramie, Texas, for her. The conversation then segued into where they'd gone to college, and the fact that, after graduation, she'd had her first business experience in Dallas, whereas he had spent ten years working in the Pacific Northwest, before coming back to his home state.

Nash helped himself to more chili. He topped it with pico de gallo, cheddar and sour cream. "How did you end up in this part of the state?"

Callie cut her son's cornbread into bite-size pieces. "My twin sister, Maggie, and I planned joint nuptials at the Double Knot Wedding Ranch on Sanders Mountain. She had second thoughts and bolted during the ceremony, so I was the only one to actually get married that day."

Nash grinned at Callie over the rim of his iced tea. "That sounds like quite a story."

Nodding, Callie returned his smile. "Maggie stayed on at the ranch after her failed wedding to work off her debt. Fell in love with their son, Hart Sanders, and his little boy, Henry. And then they eventually tied the knot." She paused. "Do you know Hart?"

Nash smiled fondly. "We go way back. I used to play with him when I was kid whenever I visited my uncle. Although, I haven't had a chance to see either Hart or his folks in the two weeks since I've been back."

Callie continued, "Hart's parents, Frank and Fiona Sanders, hired me to craft a new marketing campaign that involved utilizing social media for their wedding train business. I moved here to do that. Once I finished that, I decided to go into business for myself. Which is why I bought the one hundred acre ranch in the valley between Sanders Mountain and Echols Mountain last summer, and spent the past few months—" and almost all her savings "—turning it into a corporate retreat."

He regarded her with respect, one business person to another. His glance fell briefly to the rings on her left hand, before returning to her eyes. "How's that going?" he asked, seeming genuinely interested.

"My first event is a week from today."

A corner of his mouth twitched. "You're worried about the noise from the tree-cutting."

Callie forged ahead. "I advertise a peaceful setting for important meetings. If I don't deliver that right out of the gate…" She'd be out of business before she even got started.

Nash rubbed a hand across his jaw. He clearly hadn't shaved since morning, and the evening shadow gave him a sexy, rough-hewn allure. "How many bookings do you have?"

Seeing him push his empty plate and bowl away, Callie got up to cut them all a piece of cake. "I have four events planned from December first to December eleventh."

He thought a moment. "Are they day-only events?"

"Yes." Callie resumed her seat. "From eight in the morning till around ten in the evening, although if my clients' meetings are slow to wrap up, it could run slightly later than that."

Nash smiled, watching Brian dig into his cake. "I see where you are coming from." He leaned closer. "But here's my problem. I have been contracted to deliver four thousand fresh-cut Christmas trees by December seventh. I have a temporary crew of eighteen, coming in to help with the cutting and bundling and delivery, for the next two weeks." There was a long pause. "However, today, for a lot of reasons, we only managed to get two hundred trees ready to go. And that doesn't even include possible inclement weather because we can't cut down trees if it gets too wet. So for me to suspend operations for four whole days—"

"Would likely mean you wouldn't meet *your* business goals."

A quirk of his dark brow. "Unless…"

Trying not to think what his steady appraisal and deep voice did to her, Callie cleared her throat. "What?"

"I'm not sure it would work." His sensual lips thinned. "But…if I can get the guys to work through the weekends, including Thanksgiving Day, with the promise of equivalent days off during your events…" He paused to look her in the eye. "Would you be willing to bring in Thanksgiving dinner for everyone—if I order it and foot the bill?"

Callie was willing to do whatever necessary to facilitate peace. "I'll do better than that," she offered, beyond thrilled that they had found a solution at long last. "I'll cook. You-all can come to my ranch and have dinner there."

"I HAVEN'T SEEN you this excited since the first time you cooked dinner for Seth."

Callie turned to her twin sister. The six-months pregnant Maggie had come over with her husband, Hart, and their three-year-old son, Henry, to aid in the preparations. Currently, Hart had both Henry and her son, Brian, out riding tricycles on the sidewalk that led from the converted bunkhouse, where the meal was being prepared, to the ranch house, where she and Brian lived.

Callie carved the first of two big roasted turkeys. "The first time I cooked for Seth, it was for just him and me. Tonight, we're having twenty-four people." Hardly an intimate setting, even if her meal with Nash three evenings before sort of had been. "So if I seem a little overwrought or whatever, it's because I'm using this evening as a trial run for my first hosted corporate retreat next week."

It had nothing to do with the ruggedly handsome man heading up the team of cowboys turned temporary lumberjacks. Or the cozy dinner they'd shared. Or that this somehow carried all the emotional impact of a date. Because she wasn't dating again for a good long time. If ever.

Maggie stirred the big kettle of gravy on the stove, clearly not buying it. "Hmm."

"Plus, you know how I like to stay busy during the holidays. It just helps, not having time to think." Because it was when she let herself ruminate on the events of the past that she felt her mood fall, and she couldn't let that happen now—not when she had a child depending on her to provide the best holiday ever.

"Furthermore, just because you're happily married and expecting another baby in the spring, doesn't mean I need to be doing the same." Callie finished slicing up the first turkey and started on the second.

Maggie brought out the cranberry relish and dinner rolls, and then carried them to the long plank tables. The scent of sage dressing and freshly mashed potatoes added to the delicious aromas in the air.

"I still think you're selling yourself short," Maggie told her. "You're still young enough to marry again and have another baby or two."

And Nash Echols was definitely sexy enough, Callie thought. *If* she were looking for a mate to father more children. Which she wasn't. "The only things that concern me right now are my son and my business—"

Callie stopped at the sight of the gorgeous man in the kitchen door.

He was dressed pretty much as she'd expected. In dark jeans and a slate-gray shirt that molded his sinewy shoulders and chest and brought out the mesmerizing dark silver of his eyes. His black hair was freshly shampooed and combed, and as he strolled nearer, she caught the tantalizing scent of his aftershave lotion.

"Sorry to interrupt." Nash Echols nodded at Maggie then turned back to Callie with a genial smile. "Hart said I should just come on in."

Callie set down the carving knife and fork. Trying not to feel too excited, she wiped her hands on her apron. He was a guest…that was all. "Are the rest of the men here, too?"

His glance moved over her lazily. "They will be momentarily—if you're ready for us."

Callie fought back a reaction to all that testosterone. She jerked in a bolstering breath and returned his smile. "We are."

The question was, was she ready to spend so much time with Nash Echols—even in a group? All he'd done was walk into the spacious bunkhouse and already her heart was going ballistic.

Fortunately, the crew was right behind him.

Clearly not one to simply stand around, Nash took over the rest of the carving, while Callie pulled out big stainless-steel trays of buttermilk mashed potatoes, sweet potato casserole and green beans from the warming ovens. Maggie helped spoon hot food into serving dishes while her husband situated both little boys in booster seats. Their guests all pitched in to carry the food into the dining room.

One by one everyone found a seat. Callie took the head of the table. Nash, who had been busy filling water glasses, paused when it appeared there was only one chair left—at the other end of the long plank table. He lifted a quizzical brow her way. "Will your husband be joining us?" he asked.

IT WAS A simple question, Nash thought.

One that should have been easy to answer.

Instead, Callie froze as if that were the last thing she had expected to hear. Her twin sister and her husband exchanged long, baffled looks. Then Maggie turned back to Callie, who wasn't really meeting anyone's gaze directly, and silently telegraphed something that her twin obviously decided to ignore.

Regaining her composure, Callie flashed an overly bright smile his way. "It's just us." She gestured graciously to the chair opposite her. "So if you'll have a seat, too…"

Which begged the question, Nash thought, where was the elusive Mr. Grimes? Not that anyone else but him seemed intrigued by the matter, as grace was said, the platters of abundant food were passed around and everyone dug in. During the meal—which was, by far, the most delicious Thanksgiving dinner he'd ever had— conversation revolved primarily around the sports teams playing and the results of the games thus far.

Maggie McCabe-Sanders and her husband worked to make sure everyone felt at home. While Callie seemed happy to concentrate on making sure her son got enough to eat, and the serving platters on the table were replenished as often as need be.

Not surprisingly, by the time dessert and coffee were served, the little ones were drooping with fatigue.

Callie looked at her sister. "Would you and Hart mind…?"

Maggie smiled. "Not at all. We'll take them over to the house and get them into their pajamas."

The lumberjacks lined up to help clear the table and thank Callie for the amazing dinner, and then they headed over to Nash's ranch house next door to play cards and watch football.

Finally, it was just Nash and Callie, alone in the bunkhouse kitchen. He surveyed the tall stacks of dirty dishes while Callie picked up her buzzing cell phone. She seemed to want to sink through the floor when she caught a glimpse of the caller ID screen.

Pivoting so her back was to Nash, she said hello. Listened. With a smile in her voice said, "Of course you can. Yes, absolutely. Right now is fine. I'm in the bunkhouse."

She hung up and immediately punched in another number. "Maggie? You heard…? Oh, good. Can you keep Brian awake? Thanks." She ended the call and swung back to Nash. Bright color highlighted her elegant cheekbones.

"Company coming?" Like maybe an estranged husband?

She nodded.

"Not to worry," he said. "I'll stay here and clean all this up."

To his surprise, she looked even more panicked. "Not a good idea."

The evening was getting stranger and stranger. "Why not?"

She bit her lip. "Because—"

The door opened and a couple in their early sixties walked in. Both were eclectically dressed. The woman in a violet cashmere wrap, multicolored flowing skirt and matching blouse. An abundance of costume jewelry, a hammered silver belt and elaborately crafted Western boots completed her free-spirited look. The man wore a tapestry vest shot through with silver and gold threads, band-collared shirt, jeans and boots. A Stetson covered his free-flowing shoulder-length silver hair.

"Darling!" The woman opened her arms. Callie went into them, returning a fiercely affectionate hug, then accepted an equally warm embrace from the man.

"The place looks wonderful!" the older gentleman said.

"This retreat will be the best in Texas within the year," the woman enthused. "In fact, I'm betting it will be featured in every magazine and newspaper in the state!"

The over-the-top prediction elicited a brief, pained look from Callie. "I'd settle for just a modest success," she murmured.

"You're going to do much, much better than that," the woman insisted. "And in the process, prove all the naysayers who thought you should stay in Laramie, wrapped in widow's weeds, wrong."

Widow. Had she said *widow*?

Nash's gaze fell to the diamond and engagement rings still sparkling on Callie's left hand.

Now, this was interesting.

The older woman turned to Nash. "I'm Doris Grimes, by the way. And this is my husband, Rock. We're Seth's parents."

Nash returned the smile and stepped forward to shake hands. "I'm Nash Echols, Callie's neighbor. My men and I joined Callie and her sister's family for Thanksgiving dinner."

Callie waited until the handshaking was concluded, then intervened, "Well, I know you're anxious to see your grandson," she told her in-laws, "so you-all go on ahead. I'll be up at the ranch house as soon as I get things squared away here."

After she ushered them toward the door, they left.

Nash didn't utter a single word until Callie turned back around and met his questioning glance. "Widow, hmm?"

Pursing her lips, she angled a thumb at her sternum. "Hey, it's not my duty to correct any wrong assumptions on your part. Or anyone else's for that matter."

"So this is a common ploy? Pretending you're still married?" To do what? Drag on the grief? Keep from doing what everyone had to do eventually, which was move on…?

Callie's jaw set stubbornly as she lifted her gaze to his. "I am still married. In my heart. And always will be."

The way she had inadvertently checked him out when he walked in, and apparently liked what she saw, said otherwise. She was still a woman, and still very much alive in *every* respect, whether she wanted to admit it or not.

Not about to let her get away with deliberately misleading him, he lifted a brow. "Bull."

She blinked. "Excuse me?"

He stepped closer, purposefully invading her personal space. "You wear those rings, and let people assume you're married, to keep guys from hitting on you."

Callie drew a deep breath and stepped back. Her blue

eyes took on a cynical light. "So what if I do? In my situation you probably would, too."

"I don't go around misrepresenting myself."

"Oh, really?" she scoffed. "Because I'm pretty sure you wanted my in-laws to think you were an upstanding Texas gentleman just now."

"I *am* an upstanding Texas gentleman." Even if he had spent the past ten years in the Pacific Northwest.

"Really?" She pushed the words through gritted teeth. "Because I'm pretty sure a real Texas gentleman would not have brought up the fact that I'm a widow when it is *clearly* a subject I do not wish to discuss."

He answered her insult with a shrug, but did not disengage their locked gazes. "Fine with me," he said, just as carelessly. "I can do a search on Google on anything I want to know, anyway."

Briefly, Callie's shoulders slumped, but then she pulled herself together. Planted her hands on her slender hips. Stared at him long and hard. "Why are you so darn difficult, anyway?"

Did she really expect him to answer that? Well, turnabout was fair play, and he had a question of his own.

Why was she so damned pretty?

He'd thought she looked good the other day, when she confronted him in the woods, and again when she had showed up at his place, bearing dinner and a sweet demeanor meant to turn him pliable.

Which it had.

But it was nothing compared to the way she looked this evening, in a trim black wool skirt, tights and pleated ivory blouse. The fact she was wearing comfortable leather flats, instead of her usual heeled boots, made the seven-inch height difference between them all the more apparent.

Aware she was still waiting for some explanation as to why he took her deliberate deception so personally, he replied, "I don't like being lied to."

And he didn't like people who hung on to their grief in ways that hurt everyone else around them, either.

Callie stepped closer and leveled a withering glare on his face. "I wasn't lying." He challenged her with a raised brow.

Averting her pretty blue gaze, she mumbled, "I just didn't tell you everything you wanted to know."

Which, in turn, made him wonder. "And that is...?" he prodded casually.

She whirled away from him in a drift of perfume. "Probably that my husband died a little over three years ago in a car accident. I'd just been married a few months. I was pregnant at the time."

Nash felt for her. Losing a loved one was always hard. Especially so unexpectedly.

"And then what?" The edge was still in his voice, for a different reason now.

She walked back into the kitchen and, rolling up her sleeves, began loading dishes into the large stainless-steel dishwasher. "My family—my parents mostly—convinced me that I needed to leave Dallas and move back to Laramie, Texas, where I grew up, and be near them."

He took a stack, as well, and began loading dishes, too.

"And that's where I was," Callie continued, with a matter-of-factness that did nothing to disguise the aching loneliness in her eyes. "Until a year and a half ago when I moved here. First as marketing director with the

Double Knot Ranch, and then as owner of my own ranch and business. See? Nothing all that exciting about that. "

Finished with the plates, she began working on glasses, while he began loading the silverware.

Frustrated by her sudden silence, Nash drawled, "Which brings us to yet another problem."

Callie looked up, the pulse working in her slender throat. She rinsed her hands beneath the faucet. "Really. And what might that be?"

Nash stepped in beside her to do the same. "You're young. You're single. You're gorgeous." He leaned close enough to draw in a whiff of her hair, which was as enticing as the rest of her. "There damn sure should be something exciting going on in your life."

Callie straightened slowly.

"Let me guess." She reached for a paper towel to dry her hands. "You're just the man to give it to me."

Nash shut off the water, and once again did the same.

"Well," he said lazily, wadding up the towel and tossing it into the trash. "Since you asked so nicely." He smiled broadly. "I just might be."

Chapter Three

Callie stared up at Nash in dismay. "You wouldn't dare."

His gaze roved her face, lingering on her lips, before returning ever so slowly to her eyes. He flashed her a sexy grin, chiding, "Another thing you should never do…"

Callie caught her breath, aware she had never been around such an impossible, arrogant man. Never mind in such close quarters! "What?"

He wrapped one hand around the nape of her neck, the other flattened on her spine. Then his slate-gray eyes shuttered to half-mast as his head slowly dipped toward her. "Challenge me."

Callie shivered as his lips ghosted lightly across hers. "I'm not…" But already her eyes were closing, too. Already, she was losing herself in the feel of his hard, strong body pressed against her, the brisk wintry smell of him, the implacable masculine taste of his mouth and the resolute possession of his lips.

She thought she'd been kissed before.

She hadn't been.

Not like this.

Like he wanted to savor every iota of her heart and soul.

Yearning swept through her, fierce and undeniable.

It had been so long since she had been kissed, touched, held. So long since anyone had wanted her like this. Her whole body radiated heat and he responded by kissing her even more deeply. Unable to help herself, unable to resist the probing pressure of his lips, she surged against him. And still he kissed her, over and over again. Hard, fast. Slow, easy. Tenderly. Erotically.

Dazed, she heard a low groan wrenched from his throat, as if he wanted her beyond reason, too. It was answered by the hardening of her nipples, and lower still, the beginning of an ache that nearly rendered her senseless.

And that was, of course, when he groaned again, jerked in a breath and called a halt to their steamy fore-play.

Frustration mingled with her desire, adding to the tumultuous emotion of her day. She glared at him. "I can't believe you just did that."

He met her gaze evenly, his eyes dark, warmly assessing. "I can't, either." The corners of his mouth lifted ruefully. "I'm usually a lot more sensible. But then—" gently, he tucked a strand of hair behind her ear "—you seem to bring out the recklessness in me."

Callie let loose a rather unladylike phrase, then stepped back. "Your ego knows no bounds."

He laughed, the desire in his eyes every bit as hot and enticing as his embrace had been. He leaned close enough to press a fleeting kiss across her brow. "You could say that with some impunity if you hadn't kissed me back, Callie. Unfortunately, for *your* ego, you did."

"I DON'T SEE what the problem is," Maggie told Callie later that same evening, when everyone but the two of them had gone on to bed. Together, they carried their cups of hot apple cider into the family room and settled before the fire.

Maggie sized her sister up. "You said you were tired of being viewed as this poor tragic young widow who's constantly being handled with kid gloves."

Which was true, Callie thought, kicking off her flats and tucking her legs beneath her.

"And Nash didn't feel sorry for you," Maggie continued.

Callie sipped her cider and pointed out ruefully, "He kissed me instead."

"And that's a problem because…?" Maggie asked, grinning.

Callie closed her eyes against the sultry memory and the new flood of desire it conjured up. "I didn't want him to."

"Really?" Her sister's eyes twinkled all the more. "'Cause I think you doth protest a little too much. I mean—" she shrugged "—it's not as if he's the first guy who made a pass at you since Seth died. You handled those missteps, barely blinking an eye."

All too true. Callie rubbed at an imaginary spot on her wool skirt. "That's because…"

Maggie ventured wryly, "You didn't kiss any of them back?"

Callie paused. "How do you know that?"

"Because I'm your twin. And I know the way you think. Always have, always will, remember? Plus, I saw the way you looked at him when he came into the bunkhouse today." She waggled her brows. "Like you wanted to gobble him right up."

Callie blushed despite herself. "Okay. I admit there's a definite physical attraction there. But that's all it is."

Maggie chuckled. "You keep telling yourself that."

And Callie did.

All through the rest of her late-evening gabfest with her twin, all that night as she tossed and turned in her bed, and into the next morning. Fortunately, she had a lot to keep her busy. Breakfast to prepare for the family still gathered there, a holiday to-do list a mile long and a whole lot of distant whining chain saws in the distance to ignore.

First on the list was the purchase of two Christmas trees. As they lingered at the breakfast table, her brother-in-law listened to her plan. "Of course I don't mind driving into San Antonio to pick them up for you," Hart said. "But don't you think it's a little silly to go all that distance and drive all that way back with two trees lashed to the pickup truck when there is a perfectly reputable business selling them—likely at wholesale no less—on the ranch right next door?"

Callie had been afraid he would bring that up. Especially since she now knew that Hart and Nash were childhood friends. "Nash is not in the retail business," Callie argued.

Her former mother-in-law shrugged. "He seemed like a reasonable guy. Why don't you just ask him?"

"Or better yet, text him and see," Maggie said, still keeping an eagle eye on the two preschoolers playing in the next room.

Noticing the two little boys were beginning to get a little too rowdy, Hart went on in to supervise directly. "You have his cell phone number, don't you?" he said over his shoulder.

Callie nodded, as Hart settled onto the floor and began building a wooden block tower. Two-and-a-half-year-old Brian and three-year-old Henry immediately joined in.

"He gave it to me when we were setting up the Thanksgiving dinner," Callie admitted.

"Then...?" Maggie persisted.

Everyone stared at her, wondering why she was so reluctant to make the holiday decorating as easy as she possibly could.

Because, Callie thought, *I don't want to end up kissing him again.*

But knowing there was little chance of that, with the group of four adult chaperones at her side, she shrugged off her lingering desire and went to get her cell phone.

All eyes were upon her as she texted Nash. I need two trees. One for the house and one for the bunkhouse retreat. Can I buy them from you?

She hit Send.

Thirty seconds later, her phone chimed. No problem, Nash texted back. What size?

Twelve foot for the bunkhouse, and six foot for the ranch house, Callie typed in return.

Again, the reply coming in was nearly instantaneous. I'll get them to you this morning, Nash wrote, with the symbol for a wink. Last night was great, by the way. Especially before you kicked me out.

Reading it, Callie had to stifle a laugh but could do nothing to contain the telltale heat climbing to her cheeks.

"What?" Maggie asked, drawing nearer.

Callie shook her head and slid her phone into her pocket. "He was talking about the dinner, how much everyone enjoyed it," she fibbed. "That's all."

Maggie lifted a speculative brow.

But before anyone had another chance to say anything, a ruckus broke out in the adjacent family room. "My daddy!" Henry shouted.

"No," Brian disagreed, climbing onto Hart's lap and wrapping his arms around Hart's neck. "He's *mine*!"

Henry attempted to push his cousin aside. "No," Henry shouted back emotionally. "He is your uncle Hart. He's *my daddy*!"

Hart wrapped both boys in his arms. "Hey now," he soothed, holding them both close—to no avail. "I'm here for both of you…"

Brian let out another outraged howl, and Henry followed suit. Her heart breaking, Callie rushed to the rescue.

But Brian did not want to go with her. Or his grandparents. Or his aunt Maggie. So Callie did the only thing she could do, the thing she always did, and she went to get Brian's picture of Seth.

NASH COULD HEAR the ruckus inside, the moment he pulled up to the Heart of Texas ranch house in his pickup truck.

Inside, Nash found, it was little better. Callie was in tears. So were both preschoolers. Hart and Maggie were doing their best to separate—and soothe—the two quarreling little boys, but emotions were at an all-time high. Only Callie's in-laws were calm.

"This is exactly why you've got to think about remarrying," Doris was telling Callie.

Rock agreed. "We loved our son dearly, honey, and we will always miss him, but we know, like it or not, that life goes on. It has for us. And it must for you and our grandson, too."

Callie shook her head, understanding—if not agreeing. She wiped the moisture from her face and, picture in hand, went to her son. She hunkered down beside him. "Brian, honey, we have to talk."

The tyke turned to Callie with a heartfelt glare. "No, Mommy," he said. "No talk. No picture!" He pushed the framed photo in her hand away.

Deciding to do what he could to break the tension, Nash stepped forward and interjected brightly. "Who wants to see how many Christmas trees I have in the back of my pickup truck?" He squinted at the two boys. "I'll bet you anything you can't count them."

Henry straightened. "I can, too!" he said with importance.

Brian scrambled off Hart's lap and headed for Nash, doing his best to push his cousin out of the way in the process. "I want to see!" Brian declared.

"Well, okay then." Nash put out a hand to each child. "Let's go see. You think you fellas are old enough to see into the bed of my pickup truck, if I lift you up?"

"Yes," Henry and Brian shouted in unison.

Out the door they went. When they reached the tailgate, Nash bent down to take a boy in each arm and lifted them high. Their quarrel forgotten, they leaned over to look into the bed of his truck, where four unwrapped, fresh-cut pines, of varying sizes, lay.

"Wow," the cousins said in unison.

Nash let them study the trees. "Think we should get them out, to see just how tall they are?"

The boys nodded.

Nash handed off Brian to Callie, and Henry to Hart. "Okay then," he said with comically exaggerated importance. "Everyone stand back…"

The next few minutes were spent admiring the trees from all angles and selecting which one would go into the bunkhouse retreat and which would go to the ranch house.

By the time they secured each in the stands Callie had already purchased, the boys were filled with wonder.

"You're a lifesaver," Callie said, as she walked him back to his truck, while the others all returned to the ranch house.

Nash tipped his head at her. "Happy to be of service," he drawled.

Callie's eyes drifted to his mouth. Flushing, she sucked in a breath and returned her gaze to his. "What do I owe you for the trees?"

That was easy. "Dinner—tonight."

Her slender shoulders stiffened. "I don't think that's a good idea."

He studied the mutinous expression on her pretty face. "Why not?" he prodded, enjoying the display of temper.

Aqua-blue eyes narrowed. "Because."

He stepped close enough to inhale the flowery scent of her hair and skin. "We might end up kissing again?"

Scoffing, Callie folded her arms in front of her, tightening the cashmere fabric of her sweater over the rounded softness of her breasts. "That's not going to happen."

He moved even closer. "Mmm-hmm," he said huskily. It took everything he had not to touch her again. Haul her into his arms. And…

"And what if I promise not to kiss you again?" he asked. "At least tonight?"

A pulse throbbed in her throat. "Meaning?"

"I only like to think about things like that short term."

"Well, I don't like to think about them at all!"

He'd been able to tell that it had been a while. A long

while. "So noted," he said dryly. Besides it wasn't a vow which would necessarily be hard to keep if she continued to have as many chaperones as she had inside her home at that moment.

"Seems like your son could use the distraction," he persuaded.

He had her there…and she knew it.

Callie blew out a gusty sigh. "Fine," she conceded. "But don't expect anything other than leftovers."

Leftovers sounded a heck of a lot better than she knew.

"What time?" he asked, before she could change her mind.

Another breath, so deep it lifted—then lowered—the soft swell of her breasts.

Not that he was noticing, he told himself firmly.

She bit her lip, as she considered. "Seven-thirty?"

Nash shrugged. "Sounds good to me."

And then, before he was tempted to forgo all reason and kiss her again, he turned and walked away.

Chapter Four

Nash was surprised to see only Callie's SUV parked in front of her ranch house when he arrived Friday evening. And even more surprised to see the way she was outfitted when she opened the door to him.

"Ah," he couldn't resist teasing, "you dressed up just for me."

Callie flushed. Clearly she had meant her attire to send a message that this evening meant nothing to her. And he had to admit, on that score, she had done a fine job.

She was definitely dressed to un-impress—in old jeans and a loose-fitting blue chambray shirt, washed so many times it was soft and thin as silk, socks and moccasins, all her makeup scrubbed off.

Looking around the foyer, he realized that everyone else appeared to be gone. She had massive to-do lists spread out on the coffee table, as well as photos of her late husband and wedding pictures prominently displayed on the mantel.

Which was even more amusing, Nash noted, since none of that had been there earlier in the day.

He shrugged out of his shearling jacket and hung it on the coatrack, then followed her into the kitchen. The scent of sage dressing, turkey and cranberries wafted through the air.

"Brian asleep?"

Callie nodded, clearly disappointed about that, too. "I had hoped he would be up, but he is so overtired, it's probably for the best."

"And your in-laws?"

Another tight officious smile. "They're off to spend the weekend at the holiday craft show in San Antonio." She gestured for him to have a seat at a table set for two.

She went to the oven and pulled out casserole dishes. Turkey smothered in gravy. Potatoes and stuffing. Some sort of vegetable medley that hadn't been on the table the evening before. Warm cranberry and apple compote. A loaf of what appeared to be homemade bread. And butter.

When she had everything at the table, she sat down, too. "Rock and Doris have a wholesale Texana souvenir business. Basically they sell or make anything and everything that has to do with the history and culture of Texas. They trade with businesses all over the state, so even though they are based in my hometown, they are on the road a lot."

Nash heaped food on his plate, then dug in. "I gather they supported your decision to start your own business and move away from Laramie?"

"They did."

Her food was every bit as good the second time around. "Are your parents as understanding?"

"No," Callie admitted. "They wanted me to stay closer to home. But I still see them a fair amount, since they're both doctors, and attend a lot of medical education seminars in San Antonio."

"How do they feel about the prospect of you getting married again?"

She kept her eyes on his a disconcertingly long time, then lifted her chin. "We haven't really talked about it."

"And yet your in-laws want you to take another leap of faith, as soon as possible it would seem."

"What can I say?" Her silver Christmas star earrings jangled as she tilted her head slightly to one side. "They're hopelessly romantic. My late husband was the same."

"And you…?"

"Used to be a romantic fool," she said. The enticing curves of her breasts pressed against her blouse as she inhaled sharply. "No more."

Wishing he could give in to his desire, haul her onto his lap and lock lips with her again, Nash recalled his promise not to kiss her again tonight. "So you're not interested in getting married again?"

The mutinous light was back in her blue eyes. "Nope. Not at all. Been there, done that. See no reason to ever do it again. Or even, really, date."

Message sent, Nash thought, but not necessarily received.

He grinned, the man in him rising to the womanly challenge in her. He leaned back in his chair, his shoulders flexing against the rungs. "You're going to live your whole life without sex?"

"I didn't say that, exactly."

Now they were getting somewhere! "Then…?"

Her flush deepened, as if she knew how ludicrous she sounded. "Why are you asking me this?"

Lazily, he looked her up and down, amazed at how

gorgeous she was, under any circumstances. Aware she was waiting for an answer, he said, "I'm curious."

She studied him coolly in return. "Okay, if you must know," she said, clearly not understanding why this was so, "I could see myself having an affair—at least in theory—if I could keep it strictly as a bed-buddy, casual-sex type of thing."

This was news. "Bed-buddy," he repeated in shock.

She leveled another long, droll look. "You know. Someone you have sex with when the mood strikes, but don't have any kind of romantic attachment to."

Her matter-of-fact assertion sounded even more ludicrous the second time around.

"Or you could 'hire' a companion," he quipped. "Someone like…say, me…who would 'work for food' under those circumstances."

She shook her head at the merriment twinkling in his eyes. Knowing even without him saying so that he was already half-serious. "You're so funny."

He chuckled. "So are you."

Again it took everything he had to resist touching her.

They locked eyes, drawing out the sensually charged moment.

"You don't believe I could have a casual affair, do you?" Callie challenged. He stood and carried his dishes to the sink. "Not for one second. No."

She rose, too, her motions as graceful as they were deliberate. "Why not?"

He watched her slide the plates into the dishwasher, then ease the door back into place with more than necessary gusto. "Because you might say you've let go of your romantic ideals, but those to-do lists you had out for me to see, of everything you want to do to celebrate Christmas, say otherwise."

Callie swung toward him, her body nudging his in the process. "Those lists have nothing to do with how I feel. And everything to do with how I want *my son* to feel."

He studied the conflicted expression on her face. "I don't understand."

"The truth is…I haven't felt like celebrating Christmas since my husband died. But," she added the all important caveat, "I have a child who needs to experience all the wonder and hope and joy that the holiday can bring, so I go through the motions. For him."

"You don't think he knows that's what you're doing?"

Callie released an exasperated breath. "He's two and a half."

"So?"

Another silence fell, this one fraught with tension. "So…he can't even figure out what a daddy is. *Yet.*" Nash lounged against the counter, legs crossed at the ankle, his hands braced on either side of him. "Except that he knows he wants one and doesn't have one."

Her jaw took on the determined tilt he was beginning to know so well. "Brian will get over it."

"And if he doesn't?"

"He is going to have to," Callie insisted, looking Nash right in the eye, "because I am not going to marry again without love. And I'm not going to marry for purely romantic reasons, either."

HER WORDS WERE TRUE. Nevertheless, Callie still wished with all her heart that she hadn't said them. Hadn't revealed nearly so much about herself to the man standing opposite her.

Nash looked shocked. "So you won't marry again, period."

His low, masculine voice sent a thrill through her. "Nope." Determined to keep him at arm's length, she continued, "Once you've had the best, anything that follows is bound to be second-rate, and who wants that, right?"

His chuckle was warm and seductive. Gazing down at her, as if she had just given him the opening he needed, he turned to face her, trapping her between the counter and his big hard body. "Not even for companionship and sex?" he taunted softly.

Pretending she couldn't feel the sizzle of awareness sifting between them, she backed up as much as she could, which turned out to be about half an inch. "Why do you keep bringing the subject back around to sex?"

He remained close. Still not touching her, he shrugged. "Not sure." His gaze traced the shape of her lips before returning evocatively to her eyes. "Just seems to be on my mind whenever I'm around you."

Hers, too. She flattened her hand across his chest. "Well, stop thinking about it." Her attempt to shove him aside failed.

He remained as unmovable as a two-ton boulder. Dipping his head, he kissed the back of her forearm. "Easier said than done."

Her entire body leaped into flame. And he hadn't so much as actually touched her yet. She lifted her hand away from the hard musculature of his broad chest and the slow, steady beat of his heart. "Listen to me, Nash Echols, I am not the woman for you."

He flashed another thoughtful half smile, then lowered his head and slanted it across hers. "Actually, Callie," he said, pausing to deliver a gentle, persuasive kiss, "you might be just what I need." Hands still braced on the counter on either side of her, he kissed her again, even more provocatively this time. "And I might be just what you need," Nash persisted, trailing kisses over the nape of her neck, across her collarbone. "Since you're in the market for sex-with-no-strings-attached…"

Callie's eyes shuttered closed, but she forced them open. Forced herself to look him in the eye. "I never actually said that." Although she had been thinking it, at least whenever he was around.

His chuckle remained confident. "Speaking hypothetically is one step away from actually doing something. You know that."

Fine. So maybe the idea of going without making love again—ever—was not only depressing, it was a tad unrealistic, too, given the signals her body had been transmitting the past few days.

But not about to give him the satisfaction of being right, she squared her shoulders. "I didn't say I wanted the sex to be with you."

He looked down at her old, loose chambray shirt— seeming to visually strip her naked, to see what was beneath. "Not verbally. Physically," he looked again, as if he could tell her nipples had peaked, "you seem to be hinting at just that."

She moaned as his hands slid under her blouse, moved upward to cup her breasts. "I knew you were trouble the first day we met."

He bent to kiss her again. Slowly, tantalizingly. "But it's the kind of trouble you want to be in. Would be in, if you weren't so set on living the life of a nun."

One button was undone, then the next, and the next. "And it's a damn shame to see you so alone."

She willed herself to move, but found her legs would not cooperate. Nor would her knees. She swayed back against the counter, holding on to the edge on either side of her. "Why?"

The side of his hand moved across her collarbone, lower still, to the valley between her slowly rising and falling breasts. "Because you're young and vital and beautiful." His fingers grazed across her skin. "And, judging from your display of temper the other day, have way too much passion locked away inside."

Passion that welled up, unchecked, whenever she saw him. Passion that—like now—made her helpless to fight the desire roiling inside her. She moved her hands up to his shoulders, intending to push him away and failing. "You don't know anything about me," she whispered, looking deep into his dark silver eyes. "Not really."

He reached around behind her, unfastening her bra, caressing and claiming her beneath the sheer lace cloth. "I know," he rasped, "that widow or not, you miss being kissed. Touched. Loved."

"I do. Not—" Her words were smothered by the feel of his lips on hers.

She meant to resist him, she really did, but the heat and pressure of his mouth sent a thrill spiraling through her. For too long she'd been treated with kid gloves by everyone around her. For too long, she'd felt only half alive. Yet now, with his hands on her skin, his mouth on hers, that was no longer true. She was more alive than she had been in her entire life.

"See?" he whispered, stepping back. "That wasn't so bad, now was it?"

She exhaled slowly, wishing there were some way to discretely refasten her bra. As embarrassment and anger surged within her, she scowled at him and turned away. "I should have known you wouldn't be a gentleman for long."

He stepped behind her, fastened her up again. Then, coming around to face her, reached for the buttons on her blouse, declaring proudly, "I thought my kiss was very…gentlemanly."

She shoved his hand away and put her shirt together herself. "Erotic, yes." She looked down to make sure the buttons were in the right holes.

He chuckled. "I can go with that."

Finally, Callie was dressed again, but her breasts were still tingling. Lower still, a wildfire of need raged.

She drew a deep, bolstering breath, determined to put him in his place. "But let's be clear here. A gentleman wouldn't have kissed me at all. Especially after promising me that he wouldn't!"

Mischief danced in Nash's eyes. "You're right. It is all a little too soon. This being our third date, after all."

"*Third!*" Callie sputtered. Now she knew why she had never dated a bad boy before. They were definitely too much trouble.

"The first was the night you brought me dinner. The second, Thanksgiving."

"There were twenty-six people here, if you count my in-laws!"

"I admit it was kind of a group thing. Till after…" He waggled his brows suggestively. "Then, it was just you and me. And then of course, there's tonight. I really enjoyed tonight."

The hell of it was, so had she. From the moment he

had stepped through her front door, she had felt incredibly excited and alive. But that was neither here nor there. "You may annoy the heck out of me."

He grinned.

"But this isn't seventh grade."

"You're right." He rubbed the flat of his hand beneath the underside of his smoothly shaven jaw. "I never went to second base in seventh grade...and I suspect you didn't, either."

Ignoring that last comment, she plunged ahead. "Furthermore, I don't get involved with sexy upstarts. Never have. Never will."

His expression sobered, all but his eyes, which were still gleaming merrily. "Good to know."

Feeling like a schoolmarm in front of an unruly class, Callie lifted a lecturing hand. "From this point forward, there is not going to be anything going on between us—except cooperation of a business nature."

Nash went back to the table to claim the serving dishes. "Speaking of which...did Frank and Fiona Sanders tell you that they have invited me and my crew to join the Old-Fashioned Christmas Celebration at Sanders Mountain on December twenty-first?"

CALLIE STARED AT him in shock. "The Sanders did what?"

"Asked me to participate. They said you are organizing it."

Telling herself she had not just stumbled into a lion's den of temptation, Callie kept her eyes locked with his. "Although I no longer work full-time at the Double Knot, I still advise them part-time and help out with all the marketing."

"Is this an annual event?" he asked.

Glad to be moving back to a conversation that was strictly business, she got the last of the serving dishes and slid them into the dishwasher. "It's the first, although we're expecting it to become a beloved yearly tradition."

Nash stepped back, giving her room to work. "How did it come about?"

Callie added soap to the dishwasher and turned it on. "They don't book a lot of outdoor weddings for Nature's Cathedral in December and January—the weather is too cold for most. So I suggested that Frank and Fiona use the lag time to put on an old-fashioned Christmas Celebration for their clients, suppliers and referral partners and their families, both as a way of saying thank you and to drum up future business."

She switched off the light and he followed her into the hall. "For you, as well?"

Callie nodded. "We could do the same for your Christmas tree business."

"As well as the xeriscape plants and trees I am hoping to sell to local garden centers."

She paused next to the coatrack in the foyer. "In the meantime, you could do what I am going to do, and raffle off free trees and/or evergreen wreaths to whatever number of lucky guests you decide upon."

"How many people are you hoping to host?"

"Five hundred or so. Although invitations are going out for close to one thousand guests."

He smiled. "Impressive."

She reached for his hat and coat, and handed them to him. "We're setting up the party barn at the Double Knot as a Santa's Village. Hart is going to play Santa. We'll also have photographers, train rides up the moun-

tain and a choir and a brass quintet at Nature's Cathedral
to get people in the holiday mood."

"Sounds great."

She arched a brow. "So you're in?"

"Absolutely."

"It means you'll have to help the day of the event,
as well as the week or so leading up to it," she warned.
"Sure you're up to that?"

"No problem. As soon as I fill the orders for the
Christmas trees I already have, my schedule will free
up considerably."

They looked at each other.

Callie knew if he stayed they would only end up kissing again. She made a show of stifling a yawn.

He grinned, as if knowing however tired she might
be, sleep was going to be a long time coming. Especially
if she started thinking about the way he had kissed her,
and touched her, again…

Which, she told herself firmly, she would not.

His grin widened all the more. "I can take a hint."
He shrugged on his coat and ambled toward the front
door. "If you need anything before Monday…" he said
over his shoulder.

"I'm good, but thanks." She reached for the knob and
opened the door for him.

"Seriously." He paused, looking down at her, tenderness pushing aside the mischief in his eyes. "I'm here
for you."

Callie nodded, a lump in her throat. It had been a
long time since she had been looked after by any man.

He settled his Stetson square on his head. "This is
where you tell me you're here for me, too."

She continued looking at him, poker-faced.

He winked. "Us being neighbors and all…"

He really knew how to put a gal on the spot. Lucky for him, she'd been brought up to be a Texas lady. "I'm here for you—as a neighbor—too," she said finally.

He looked like he'd won the lottery. "Just what I wanted to hear."

To her surprise, she felt like she had won it, too.

"In the meantime," he went on, stepping over the threshold, "it's supposed to rain tomorrow. So we probably won't be working."

Callie lounged in the doorway, arms crossed, aware he had planned for weather delays.

"So if you and Brian are up for it," Nash continued genially, "I was going to see—"

Callie held up a hand, cutting him off. "Actually, we already have a get-together planned for tomorrow. But maybe some other time?" For a moment, Nash looked like he wanted to say something else. Then he stopped himself, nodded. "Some other time, then," he said.

And, looking more cheerful than ever, left.

Chapter Five

"Bad day?" Maggie asked, when Callie and Brian showed up at her home the following afternoon.

"Unbelievably bad so far." She carefully hung up their rain-spattered coats on the tree in the hall. Then watched her son stomp off to join his cousin in the family room, where Hart was busy setting up a child-size table and chairs.

It had been one temper tantrum after another since the moment Brian had gotten up that morning. And, as it turned out, the steady, pouring rain and ever-present gloom hadn't helped either of their moods.

Maggie hugged Callie as tightly as her pregnant-form would allow. "Well, this, too, shall pass," she promised cheerfully. "At least that's what Hart and I tell ourselves whenever Henry is overtired and out of sorts."

Appreciating the support, Callie smiled, then took a moment to admire the decorations her sister and her husband had put up. A beautiful wreath hung on the front door, and a big tree in front of the bay window dominated the formal living room. Garlands laced the staircase, stockings the mantel. Colored lights and a Santa sleigh and reindeer set adorned the exterior of the house.

Clearly, they had gone all out. Which only reminded her of the work she had yet to do.

The trees Hart had previously delivered for the bunk-house and her home remained undecorated. As did the rest of the interior of her home. Callie bit her lip, wondering when she was going to find the time to get everything done.

Drawing a deep breath, she moved farther into the house. "Anyone else here yet?"

Maggie shook her head. "You're the first. Although the cookie dough I made is ready to roll out."

Callie carried the two containers of spritz dough, baking sheets and the cookie press she'd brought with her into the kitchen. "Mine is ready to go, too."

Before they could talk further, the doorbell rang, again and then again. The other two couples came in out of the rain, their preschoolers in tow. Callie was still saying hello to the other four adults when the doorbell rang a third time.

Hart went to get it.

"Hey, buddy," her brother-in-law said cheerfully. Callie turned, and her heart did a little somersault in her chest as she came face-to-face with Nash Echols. What in the world was he doing here? At a gathering of preschool kids and their parents, no less?

"Glad you could make it," Hart told Nash, slapping him on the back.

Recognition dawned. Suddenly, she had to know. "Was this what you were talking about last night?" Callie asked Nash, moving closer. When he had off-handedly tried to make plans with her for today, then backed off without ever saying what it was he had been wanting to do?

Nash took off his jacket and hung it up. He was wearing jeans and a gray-and-black-plaid flannel shirt that brought out the dark silver of his eyes Beads of water clung to his face and shone in his hair. Once again, he had shaved closely.

"Yeah. I was going to offer you and Brian a ride, but I could see you wanted to drive yourself." His glance moved over her lazily, appreciatively taking in her cowlnecked sweater and jeans. "And if it hadn't rained, as predicted, I wouldn't be here."

He would have been working on the mountain cutting down trees with the rest of his crew, Callie knew.

He regarded her affably. "So, I figured we'd just each do our own thing."

Which, for Callie, now included feeling warm and tingly all over…

Oblivious to her overtly sensual reaction to their guest, her brother-in-law urged Nash forward. "The Texas game's on. Come on in, let me introduce you to everyone," Hart said. The two men headed off to the family room.

Callie sighed with relief and made a beeline for the kitchen. Taking advantage of the momentary privacy, Callie whispered to Maggie, "Is this a fix-up?"

Her twin scoffed and adjusted the racks in the double convection ovens so three pans of cookies could be baked in each simultaneously. "No."

"Really?" Callie countered. "Because everyone else here is married, except Nash and me, and everyone has a child in the Country Day Montessori Preschool, except Nash. So…"

Maggie pulled an apron out of a drawer and handed

it to Callie. "It's just the holidays can be a hard time to be alone," she explained.

Callie knew that better than anyone. Still… Starting any kind of romantic dalliance, no matter how causal, this time of year wasn't wise, either. And if Nash were equally at loose ends—because he had just moved to the area—then it was a doubly bad idea.

"Surely he has family somewhere," she protested, wishing she weren't so attracted to him. Because it would have made things a whole lot easier if she hadn't wanted to kiss him again.

Maggie got a funny look on her face as her glance drifted to a point behind Callie. "Actually—" she stammered.

"My parents live in Japan these days," Nash said, joining them at the kitchen island. He helped himself to a can of soda, then lounged against the counter, making himself at home.

Callie luxuriated in the warmth radiating from his tall, strong body. "They don't come back for the holidays?"

Setting the can down, he folded his brawny arms across his powerful chest and kept his glance trained on hers. "Nope."

She waited. To her frustration, no other information was forthcoming. "I'm sorry," she said finally.

His gaze remained steady.

She couldn't help but notice the smile on his mouth did not reach his eyes.

"No reason to be," he continued matter-of-factly. "My folks don't really like Christmas anyway so it's not like I'm missing much by not being with them."

"How could anyone not like Christmas?" Polly, one

of the other mothers, asked as she came in to join the conversation.

"Long story," Nash said, taking a long swig of soda.

And definitely not one he planned to elaborate on, Callie noted.

After quenching his thirst, Nash rubbed his hands together and grinned. "So, ladies, what can I do to help?"

The last thing Callie needed was Nash underfoot. Especially when he was looking and smelling so good. Like the middle of a forest after a hard winter rain.

Luckily, her twin jumped in to help Callie get the space she needed.

Maggie took Nash's elbow and steered him toward the adjacent family room, where cheers and sports commentating could be heard. "We're still trying to get set up in the kitchen, so if you want to help the other guys watch the kids…"

"And catch the second half of the football game?" he teased.

"Well—" Maggie smiled, like the gracious hostess she was "—there is that."

Nash ambled off.

And for a while, all was good. Callie and Maggie filled cookie sheets with dough and slid them into the oven to bake, while the two other mothers set up a decorating station with various frostings and sprinkles for the kids.

They were just ready to call the kids in to do their thing, when a ruckus broke out in the other room. "I sit on *my* daddy's lap," Petey announced loudly. He climbed up on Phil.

"I sit on mine!" Henry clamored up to give Hart a hug.

"This is my daddy," Bobby stated proudly, climbing onto Ted's lap.

Once again, Callie noted, her son, Brian, was the odd man out.

And once again, her next-door neighbor injected himself into the calamity that was her life.

Nash hunkered down beside Brian. "Hey," he said to the little boy in mock indignation. He thrust out his lower lip in a parody of a toddler tantrum and angled his thumb at the center of his broad chest. "I don't have anyone to sit on my lap!"

Brian immediately sympathized. He laced his arms about Nash's strong shoulders, volunteering importantly, "I do it!"

"Well, thanks, buddy." Nash scooped Brian into his arms, stood and carried him over to an armchair.

Before Callie could do so much as send Nash a grateful glance, her son looked into Nash's eyes and asked loudly enough for everyone in the room to hear, "Are *you* my daddy?"

No, NASH THOUGHT, feeling the weight of the adorable little boy in his arms, *but at this moment I'd sure like to be.*

Before he could respond, Callie rushed forward, a stricken expression on her face. She handed her son a pocket-size version of the same photo she had shown him the day before. "Seth is your daddy," she reminded gently.

Brian scowled and shoved the photo away. "Don't want heaven!"

Nash couldn't blame the little boy. Knowing a loved one was in an unreachable place far away was no comfort at all. Although he didn't blame Callie. She had to tell her son the truth about Seth from the get-go. Especially now that Brian was old enough to start noticing other kids had dads around to love them, when he did not.

"Want *this daddy*," Brian continued, wrapping his arms around Nash's neck and snuggling close.

Callie flushed all the more. "Honey, Nash is not your daddy."

"I'm your friend," Nash added.

"Friend *and* daddy," Brian bartered with perfect two-and-a-half-year-old logic. He squinted up at Nash, persisting, "Like story…?"

Nash had no clue what Brian was talking about. Nor did anyone else. Except Callie, whose cheeks went from hot pink to sheer red. "I think he's talking about one of his favorite storybooks. It's about a baby bird, who is looking for his mom, and asks all the other animals if they are his mother before he finally finds her…" Her voice trailed off.

Suddenly, all the other parents seemed to know what she was talking about, Nash noted, as they nodded their heads in unison.

"Yeah, that's a great one," Polly said.

Appearing happy someone understood where his question came from, Brian turned back to Nash.

"Are you my daddy?" the little boy asked again, even more determinedly.

Really seeming to mean, Nash thought, *will you* be *my daddy?*

And he had absolutely no idea what to say to that.

Luckily, the team they had been rooting for scored. A cheer went up on the TV, along with excited chatter from the sports announcers and lots of on-field celebration by the players. Everyone, including the children, were momentarily distracted by the on-screen commotion.

Callie wasted no time clapping her hands together. "Okay, boys! Is everyone ready to decorate the cookies for the firemen and the policemen?"

When enthusiastic shouts filled the air, Maggie and the other moms shepherded the kids toward the kitchen. Callie paused to shoot Nash a grateful look, then went to join the others.

The rest of the afternoon went smoothly.

And, to Nash's relief, Brian seemed to forget all about wanting a daddy who was not in heaven.

He decorated the cookies with cheerful zeal, and then played well with the other kids and the adults present. By dinner time, though, the little boy was sagging with exhaustion and looking on the verge of another meltdown.

And though Maggie and Hart invited them all to stay for dinner, to Nash's disappointment, Callie declined the invitation and coaxed Brian into his coat with the promise of his favorite music on the drive home.

Dutifully, the two said goodbye to everyone, then Brian came back to give Nash an extra hug. His heart swelling, he crouched down to accept it. Damn, the little fella sure was cute.

"Friend *and* daddy," Brian declared stalwartly, looking Nash right in the eye while patting his arm.

Nash wished.

CALLIE HAD JUST settled Brian into his toddler bed when the doorbell rang. Pausing to adjust the covers over his contentedly sleeping form, she went downstairs. A look through the viewer confirmed her suspicion.

She swung open the door. Nash stood on the portal,

looking handsome as ever in a sheepskin coat and Stetson. He had a large take-out bag from a popular Tex-Mex restaurant in his hand, a hopeful grin on his ruggedly chiseled face, the rain still pouring down in sheets behind him.

This made it the third evening in a row he had shown up at dinnertime.

And though she knew she shouldn't be happy to see him, she secretly was.

"I took a chance you hadn't had dinner yet," he drawled.

Deciding not to make things too easy for him, Callie lounged in the portal and folded her arms in front of her. "Depends on whether you count a bite of my son's macaroni and cheese."

He mimed horror. "Definitely not."

Because the aromas coming from the bag smelled too good to resist, she stepped back to usher him inside. "Come on in."

He took off his hat and flashed her a sexy grin. "Don't mind if I do."

"So you didn't stay for dinner at Maggie and Hart's, either, I guess?"

His hand brushed hers as he handed her the bag. "A little awkward, don't you think? Me being the only single adult left?"

She sighed, knowing all too well what it was like to be included out of duty or pity…or both—especially at this time of year. "People mean well."

He took the bag from her, their fingers brushing again, and followed her into the kitchen. "I know. And I do appreciate the sentiment behind the gesture."

"So why did you really show up there today? And

don't tell me that it was the football, because you didn't seem all that interested in the on-field action to me."

"Hey, I went to Texas A&M, so to root for the Texas Longhorns…"

"Would be blasphemy, I know. But you didn't answer my question. Why did you show up there today?"

He flashed her another smile. "You."

She studied his handsome face and tall, muscular frame. He was who he was, take it or leave it. She tried not to think how much they had in common that way. "You felt sorry for me?"

"I wouldn't say pity entered into it. At all."

Oh, dear. Telling herself she needed to be driven more by practicality than emotion, she said, "So if not pity, then…?"

His gaze turned tender. "I want to get to know you," he said softly. "And Brian, too."

Now she was *really* in trouble.

Callie cleared her throat. "Speaking of which…I do owe you for coming to our rescue before."

He lent a hand as she began to set the table for two. "No problem."

"So what's this?" He pointed to the to-do list labelled For Brian's Christmas that she had left on the kitchen table.

"A compilation of all the activities I have planned for him in December."

Nash picked up the list and read, "Go to see Santa. Take a tour of the lights. Help decorate the gingerbread house. Figure out a way to see snow. Bake cookies. Go caroling. Decorate the tree. Make presents—"

"I thought it would be more meaningful than buying something."

"Wrap presents."

"He can help."

Nash handed it back to her, clearly not as impressed as she would have hoped. "That's a pretty ambitious list."

Callie nodded, sober now. "I figure if I can keep Brian busy enough he won't have time to think about not having a daddy." At least that was the plan.

"And what will staying this busy do for you?" Nash asked.

Good question, Callie thought. "It will help me get through the holidays." With my heart intact.

He studied her through narrowed eyes. "Is that all you want? Just to *get through* the holidays? Not really enjoy them?"

Callie gave him a droll look, not surprised he was back to challenging her again. "Of course I want to enjoy them." With a beleaguered sigh, she pulled several tinfoil trays with cardboard lids and heating instructions from the bag, as well as a bag of chips and containers of queso and salsa. "What I don't know is, what I am going to do about Brian's desire for a daddy."

Solemn now, too, Nash asked, "What do you mean?"

Glad she had someone who could be objective to talk with this about, Callie reached into the fridge and pulled out two long-necked bottles of Texas-brewed beer and a single lime. While she quartered the lime, Nash twisted off the caps. Finished, she traded a beer for a lime wedge. "I've tried and tried to explain to him that Seth is in heaven, but he just doesn't get it." With a frown, Callie pushed the lime down into the beverage and watched as Nash did the same.

They clinked bottles in a wordless toast and took a sip. Because Nash was so understanding, she went on, "I put a photo of Seth next to Brian's bed. And I carry a laminated one in my purse for him to look at whenever the subject comes up. Which recently has been a lot. I've even read him this storybook about it."

Callie slid the dinners into the oven to warm, then went off, returning with the aforementioned picture book. "I've read this book to him and told him what a wonderful place heaven is…that he will see his daddy there one day, when it's time." Her throat suddenly began to ache, and she took another small swallow of beer. "But he doesn't want to hear it."

Nash opened up the fresh bag of tortilla chips, then the dips. "He is pretty young."

"I know that." Callie scooped some warm, savory melted cheese with tomato, jalapeno and onion onto a crispy tortilla chip. "I don't expect him to understand the finality of death. The fact is that children don't really begin to comprehend that until they are at least eight years old. But I do know that Brian can hear a story, get the gist of it and recall it later. Even apply the facts of it to something else."

Nash sat opposite her, his knees nudging hers beneath the table. "Like the search for a mommy morphs into the search for the daddy."

Callie sighed and rested her chin on her hand. "Right."

Nash reached over and tucked a strand of hair behind her ear. "He's pretty smart for a two-and-a-half-year-old."

"As well as determined." Callie sighed and sat back. She pulled the edge of the paper label from the bottle, then gave up when it refused to budge more than a quarter inch.

Once again, she leveled her gaze on Nash. "I just don't know how to give my son what he needs."

He reached across the table and took her hand in his. "I think you already are. You love him. You care for him." He made an inclusive gesture at the cozy environment. "And provide for him." Then he pointed to her holiday to-do list for her son. "And he's certainly not short on new experiences."

Callie bit her lip. "But I still can't give him a daddy."

And Brian was unwilling to settle for less.

"Yet." Their gazes met, held. "One day you will," Nash promised.

Callie smiled, despite herself. "You seem awfully sure of that," she noted wryly.

He regarded her with utter certainty. "A woman as beautiful and talented as you are is not going to stay single for long, wedding rings still on her finger or not."

"Somehow I knew you'd get around to bringing that up," she shot back. Then paused to let her next words sink in. "And no, I'm not going to stop wearing them." Blushing, she got up to check on dinner, even though she knew it wasn't quite heated through yet.

Nash tilted his head to one side. "I figured as much."

But it didn't seem to deter him, Callie noted.

Not at all.

Chapter Six

"So, not so much as a good-night kiss?" Maggie asked when she and Callie chatted on the phone the next day. In the distance, the whine of power saws continued unabated. Nash Echols and crew had been working since shortly after dawn.

Imagining they would go until dark, Callie replied, "No. We just ate and talked, and then he told me to call him if I needed anything and headed out."

"At least tell me you enjoyed yourself."

Enjoyed herself hadn't been the half of it, Callie thought. She had loved every second she spent with him. Even when he was challenging her on the fact she still wore her wedding rings.

Speaking of which…Callie looked down at her left hand. It had been itchy and uncomfortable since she had gotten up that morning. The irritation seemed the worst on the third finger of her left hand.

"Have you ever had a rash around your rings?" she asked her twin.

"Only that one time, when the guy I was dating in high school gave me a fake-silver-finish friendship ring. Remember? It turned my finger green?"

Callie laughed, thinking back to their relatively stress-free childhood. "I do, actually."

"Why? Do you have a problem?"

"Not really." Callie brushed it off. "I think my hands are just dry from the winter weather. I'll put some extra hand cream on. That should take care of it."

"So…are you ready for your first event tomorrow?" her twin asked.

Callie smiled. At least one thing in her life was going exactly the way she had planned. "Yes, I am." The bunk-house was already set up for the eight executives and their staff.

"I'll pick up Brian at preschool and keep him over-night, the way we agreed."

"Okay. But let me know if there are any problems," Callie told her. "The meeting will break up around 9:00 p.m., so if Brian can't settle down to sleep, I can come and get him then."

"Will do," Maggie promised. "And, Callie? Good luck!"

As it turned out, luck was not needed. The group arrived on time, was relatively undemanding and left shortly before eight that evening.

Nash had kept his word, too. There hadn't been a single inkling of any tree-cutting the entire day.

Happy everything was proceeding smoothly once again, Callie called her sister to see how things were going with the boys. She was relieved to learn they had gone to bed at seven and fallen asleep right away. Maggie urged Callie to enjoy the night off. Callie promised to do so, thanked her sister and hung up the phone. She looked around another long moment.

The evening stretched ahead of her.

Without Brian there, without Nash just dropping by, the house was suddenly oddly quiet.

In that instant, Callie realized she had never felt lonelier in her life.

Which meant there was only one thing to do. She released a determined sigh. *Get back to work.*

A HALF MILE down the road, Nash was just stepping out of the shower when he heard the email notification on his laptop ring. Wrapping a towel around his waist, he padded into the bedroom and saw the message from Callie. Instead of writing her back, he picked up the phone instead. She answered on the second ring, her voice every bit as soft and alluring as he recalled.

More enamored of her than ever, he said, "You wanted to talk to me about the Christmas Festival?"

"I know it's another three weeks away, but I really need to get information about your business, so I can put together a brochure showcasing everything Echols Mountain has to offer. Is there some time in the next day or two you can meet with me in person?"

His spirits rose. "How about right now?" he asked, opening his bureau drawer.

"Sure, why not. You want to come here?"

He grabbed his boxer briefs and socks. "Be there in ten."

It was more like seven. Three of which were spent driving from his ranch to hers.

Callie opened the door wide. Her hair was a silky cloud of dark curls that ended just above the nape of her neck. Smiling appreciatively, wishing he could haul her into his arms right then and there, his eyes drifted down over her delectable curves. She was clad in a red sweater dress that covered her from neck to knee, and sheer panty hose adorned her spectacular legs. A pair of big fluffy reindeer slippers covered her small, dainty feet.

He grinned. "Like your shoes."

She facetiously modeled her footwear. "Brian and Henry picked them out for me last Christmas. They were so comfy I've made them my official holiday slippers."

For someone who claimed not to be able to really celebrate Christmas, she sure looked happy now. Nash shrugged out of his coat and hung it on the rack. He ran his fingers through his still-damp hair. "Speaking of Christmas, what's that incredible smell?"

"Gingerbread." She grinned and walked him into the kitchen. "I'm trying to get the underlying cardboard house assembled tonight, too."

He knew nothing about either baking or constructing the traditional confection. However, it didn't mean he wasn't willing to lend a hand. "How's it going?" he asked casually.

She looked at the collapsed cardboard walls of the chalet-style building. "Not all that well, as you can see. Any ideas how we could stabilize it?"

Nash moved nearer. In the process he got a whiff of the flowery shampoo she used in her hair. Turning his attention back to the matter at hand, he studied the flaws for a moment. "I think I would double or triple up on the cardboard frame, and use a stronger tape to hold it all together."

"Okay, I'll gather up what we need from my office. In the meantime, how about you have a seat and go through some of these marketing brochures." She handed him a clear plastic storage box, her delicate fingers briefly brushing his in the process. "Pick out a few that appeal to you."

There was an impressive selection. All sizes, colors, fonts. Even the presentation seemed different in all. To the point if she displayed them all, side by side on a rack, each one would still stand out as unique. "Did you do all of these?" he asked.

"Mmm-hmm." She disappeared, and then came back with tape, scissors and extra cardboard. She disassembled the house, then began tracing the individual pieces she'd already made onto other pieces of cardboard with a pencil. "I'm putting together brochures for the local businesses participating in the festival. They'll be tucked into the gift baskets the guests take home with them."

Finished, she cut out the identical cardboard components along the previously traced lines.

He slid his glance to her once again. "What kind of information do you want?"

Another small, inviting smile. "Whatever you'd like to include. How you came to own Echols Mountain, for instance."

"My great-uncle Ralph Echols was like a grandparent to me. As a young kid, my family visited him every summer. When I got older, I spent longer periods at the ranch, even worked there from time to time."

"Did you always want to be in the tree business?" she asked curiously.

"I started thinking about it when I was about eighteen. My uncle said if I was serious, I needed to get a degree in forestry—which I did—and then spent ten years working in the industry in forest management." He paused. "I saved every penny I could while I was working in the Pacific Northwest. I was just getting ready to come back to Texas for good when my uncle died and left the place to me."

"Do you have any plans for the mountain besides selling Christmas trees and landscape plants?"

"I want to selectively harvest some of the pine for furniture and flooring companies, while keeping conservation in mind."

"In other words, you can't cut down too much."

"Or too little." As his uncle had, toward the end.

"Do you think you could write a few paragraphs explaining that in layman's terms? Because honestly, I think that is a pretty major selling point for your business."

"Sure."

Nash picked out a couple of small brochures with color photos. All the while, he thought long and hard about what the ranch meant to him, how it had only been known for providing Christmas trees in the past—and for the past five years, not even that.

"Maybe I could take some pictures of the mountain, too? Show how the forest has evolved during the time it lay fallow? How, as a business, we can take advantage of that to make the woods even more productive while remaining environmentally sound?"

"That's *exactly* the kind of information I need to have to devise a solid marketing brochure for you," Callie enthused, just as the kitchen timer went off. After removing the gingerbread pans from the oven, she returned to the table, where the eight triple-cardboard pieces sat, ready to assemble. Her lips twisted ruefully. "Now, if I could just get the house walls to remain upright, instead of collapsing in on their sides…"

Glad to have something to do rather than just sit there while she worked, he grinned. "Let me help you."

Finding it easier to work standing up, they carried the pieces to the kitchen counter. Nash held them in place while Callie cut and pressed the tape. When the last piece of roof went on, Nash let go. So did Callie.

She grinned as she realized it really was standing. "I don't know if it will withstand hurricane force winds... or even the weight of the gingerbread cake slabs, but..."

"Well, there's one way to find out," he drawled. Winking mischievously, he bent down and pretended to see if he could blow it over.

"No!" Callie cried. Laughing, she tugged at his arm and pulled him upright so quickly and carelessly their bodies collided. The softness of her breasts pressed into the wall of his chest. Lower still, she was just as malleable and feminine.

Just that swiftly, the playful contact turned into something else. She looked into his eyes. He looked into hers. And then did what he had been wanting to do ever since the last time he'd held her in his arms.

CALLIE KNEW NASH was going to kiss her. Knew all the reasons why she shouldn't let him. However, her will to resist faded when his mouth covered hers. Throwing caution to the wind, she rose on tiptoe and pressed her lips to his. They were hot and supple, wickedly sensual and possessive. His body tautening, he drew her closer yet. His hands slid down her spine, flattening her against him and guiding her deep into his embrace. And still his tongue explored her mouth, laying claim to her inner recesses, again and again, until passion swept through her and she released a small moan. Of pleasure. Of need. Of the wish to be closer.

She had never given much thought to her own needs. Her own desires. But being with Nash made her want to change all that. He made her want to do something for herself, instead of just everyone else. He made her want to give in to the moment, just for a little while. Explore the proof of his desire. She arched against him, wanting and needing so much. To be held. Touched. Kissed. Loved. And though love, per se, wasn't exactly in the equation, a feeling of femininity swept through her, intensifying the yearning she felt deep inside. She wrapped her arms around him, holding him so close they were almost one, her pulse pounding, her breasts rising and falling with each breath she took.

"Callie," he whispered against her mouth.

Reluctantly, she drew back and opened her eyes. Said what was on her mind. What she refused to let encompass her heart. "Let's go upstairs."

NASH KNEW HE was going to make love to her. He just hadn't figured it would be tonight. He was pretty sure from the stunned, yet somehow dreamy, expression on her face, she hadn't bargained on it, either. And that, more than anything, gave him pause.

"Callie," he said again. Not wanting this, or anything about them, to be something she might later come to regret.

She lifted his hand to her lips, kissed the back of it. "I'm not going to pretend I don't want you. When I do." Releasing a tremulous breath, she continued, "And since the times I have without my son are few and far between…"

She didn't have to say more.

He swung her up into his arms. "Which way?"

"Upstairs... First bedroom on the right."

It was, as he would have half expected, a feminine haven. With a four poster bed, pale blue silk bed-linens, romantic chaise. Soothing neutral walls. Plush carpet.

He set her down next to the bed. Still thinking she might have changed her mind.

Instead, her hands went to the hem of her sweater dress. Swept it up over her head. It hit the floor. The panty hose followed. Then the red lace-edged slip. Clad in bikini panties and matching bra, she turned back the covers and sat on the edge of the bed.

She regarded him boldly. "You next."

He knew her striptease had been part of a statement. She was an adult. She wanted sex-with-no-strings. She wanted it now. And she wanted it with him.

So he gave her an equally matter-of-fact show in return. Stripping off his boots, socks, shirt, jeans. And then, for good measure, removed his boxer briefs.

Her eyes widened. "Oh. My..."

Oh my was right. He sat down beside her, unclasped her bra and let that fall to the floor. The instant he lay her back on the sheets, her hands went to the elastic of her panties. He caught her fingers in his. "That can wait."

He stretched out beside her, lowered his head and kissed her again. Slowly. Reverently. Until her lips were wet and swollen from his kisses. Her hair tousled, her cheeks pink. He shifted her back against the pillows, gathered her breasts in both hands and lifted the lush flesh to his mouth. She sighed in pleasure as he laved the tight buds with his tongue. Knowing this was the surest way to make her feel the connection between them, he kissed his way down her body, across her abdomen, to the apex of her thighs, her navel and back again. Needing her accessible, he swept off her panties, and then found the sweetest, silkiest part of her.

She arched and caught his head in her hands. Perspiration beaded her body, lower still moisture lined the insides of her thighs. She whimpered low in her throat and gave him full rein. He suckled the silky nub and stroked inside her, fluttering his tongue. Her back arched and her thighs fell even farther apart. She quivered as he cupped her bottom with both hands, rose and penetrated her slowly. She closed around him, like a wet hot sheath.

"Nash," she whispered, wreathing her arms around him, her entire body shivering with need. He kissed her hard, still thrusting, claiming, feeling a little like a conqueror who had just captured the fair maiden of his dreams. She arched up to meet him, her response as true and unashamed as he had hoped it would be. He plunged and withdrew, aware of every soft, warm inch of her, every moan, every whimper, every clear declaration of need.

Until there was no more waiting, no more delaying, only the pleasure, only each other. And he went free-falling into the sweet and sexy oblivion right along with her.

AFTERWARD, NASH FELT her pull away. In less than a minute, Callie sat on the edge of the bed, released a sigh and buried her face in her hands. "It's not in me to be reckless."

And yet she'd climaxed nevertheless. As had he...

"But I guess I shouldn't be surprised." Her chin set

with customary determination, she got up and wrapped herself in a thick, luxurious, pale blue robe.

Although it covered her from neck to ankle, she only managed to look sexier. Maybe because he knew she was still naked—and quivering slightly—beneath.

She found a brush and restored order to her short, chin-length curls. And continued her litany of excuses, "It's Christmas. I was on a high from having successfully hosted my first executive retreat. And—" she sighed again, even more loudly this time "—I'm lonely. At least in the sense of—"

"Having someone to make love with," he guessed.

She nodded briefly, but did not meet his gaze.

He continued, a tad more cynically, "Hence you ended up in bed with me."

"Right." Callie paused, the edge of her teeth raking across her plump lower lip. She swung back to face him, her troubled gaze searching his face. "I imagine you're a little lonely, too, having just moved to the area."

Nash would have been insulted, had he not just made love with her, and known—firsthand—how completely she had given herself to him. How completely he had made love to her in return.

He rose lazily. Picked up his clothing. Began to dress. "Or in other words, your kicking me out now is nothing personal," he said, his tone as suddenly matter-of-fact as hers.

She drew a deep, bracing breath and flashed a weak smile. "Of course not."

He shrugged on his shirt and, still holding her flushed face firmly in his sights, began to button. "It's the holiday season."

"And why we shouldn't be alone," she swallowed, "with each other."

The slight catch in her voice revealed more than she knew. He sat down on the edge of the mussed covers of her bed and tugged on his boots.

She came closer, her fingers working the ends of her snugly tied belt. She looked guilty, upset, contrite and unapologetic, all at once. "This wouldn't have happened with anyone else."

Nash was not sure why he was so irked. He had known from the outset, when he'd allowed himself to follow her up here, that it would end this way. He stood. "Good to know."

She caught his arm before he could brush past her. "Nash."

At the imploring nature of her touch, his whole body tensed. He looked down at her, jaw set. "I get it. You'd rather we not do this again."

She dropped her hold. Stepped back. Gave him a beseeching glance. "We live next door to each other. We have to work together. I don't want things to be... awkward."

He snorted. "A little too late for that, don't you think?"

Silence fell as their gazes met again.

Callie leaned back against the bureau, arms folded at her waist. "Can't you just accept that I'm confused?"

He shook his head in silent admonition. "You're not the only one."

"I want to go back to being friends."

Was that what they were? He'd felt they were on the verge of a lot more than that. "Of the strictly platonic variety," she added hastily.

The practical side of Nash knew he should say yes to

whatever she wanted and get the heck out of there, now. Before the situation got any more complicated. Instead, he followed his instincts once again. Slowly but surely closed the distance between them, drew her close and kissed her slowly, lingeringly, until she melted against him. As he enfolded her tighter in his arms, her right hand encircled his neck, her left hand—the one with the rings still on it—splayed helplessly across his chest.

Once again, he reluctantly lifted his head. "If that doesn't show you we're way past platonic," he told her gruffly, "I'm just going to have to try harder. In the meantime…" He looked pointedly down at the red skin glowing, bright as Rudolph's nose, beneath her wedding and engagement rings. "If I were you, I'd really see what I could do about that."

Chapter Seven

The next morning, Callie held her hand up to the camera on her computer screen. "Do you have any idea what this is?" she asked her mom.

Lacey McCabe responded to Callie with the same care and concern she showed her pediatric patients. "It's contact dermatitis."

Glad they could Skype, since her mom was a hundred miles away, Callie countered practically, "But my rings have never bothered me before. What's changed?"

Lacey's glance narrowed, as she continued studying the picture of Callie's hand on her computer screen. "Is it possible you got some soap or some other substance stuck on the inside of the bands?"

"I don't know. Maybe. All I know is it itches like crazy and it seems to be getting worse."

"Do you have the rash anywhere else?"

"No."

Her mom paused. "It could be stress-related, too."

"But only on my ring finger, beneath my rings?" Callie said skeptically.

Lacey's dad appeared beside her mom. He, too, was getting ready to go to the hospital for morning rounds. "Looks like contact dermatitis to me," he concurred.

"What should I do for it?" Callie asked.

"First, take off your rings and take them to the jewelers to be professionally cleaned to make sure there is nothing on the inside of the bands or stuck anywhere in the setting," her mom said. "Then leave the rings off until the rash goes away."

"And in the meantime?" Callie pressed, aware her finger had started to itch like the devil again.

Her dad volunteered, "You might try putting a little petroleum jelly or fragrance-free moisture cream on it to form a protective barrier over the irritated skin. And then wrap the area with a couple of bandages, or some gauze and waterproof tape, so nothing else can rub up against it."

"And be sure you don't get any soap on the area until the rash has cleared." Her mom added earrings and a necklace to her ensemble. "So if you need to wash it, do so only with plain water."

"It should be better in a day or so," her dad assured her.

"But if it's stress-related, it could take a little longer than that," her mom cautioned as she pulled a cardigan over her blouse and paused to adjust the collar. "I wouldn't worry about it unless it spreads past the irritated area. Or gets a lot worse."

"If it does, call us." Her dad knotted his necktie then slipped on his suit jacket. "We'll hook you up with a dermatologist in San Antonio."

"Thanks, Mom, Dad," Callie said.

"Is everything else okay?" Her mom paused, intuitive as ever. "Anything else we should know about?"

They certainly didn't need to know she'd lost all judgment and had slept with Nash Echols the night before!

"Not a thing," Callie said merrily, doing her best to affect a Christmas cheer she still didn't really feel.

Her mom squinted into the Skype camera. "Like a new boyfriend?"

Callie drew a deep breath, as her depression turned to sheer nerves. "I don't know where you got that idea."

Her parents exchanged glances, then her dad said, "Maggie said something about a friend of Hart's last time we talked. Nash Heckles?"

"Echols," Callie corrected, pretty sure Dad had confused the last name on purpose. "And there's nothing there." *That I'm going to call home about anyway.*

Her mother's expression gentled. "Well, just be careful, honey. This can be a hard time of year, you know."

Her dad nodded. "It can be easy to mistake loneliness for something else."

Like lust? Or the possibility of falling in love? Callie told herself she had a handle on the first, and nothing to worry about regarding the second issue. "I know," she said, in a hurry to cut the conversation short before her folks could scout out anything else. "Listen, I've got to go and pick up Brian. He spent the night with Maggie last night—because the event here ran late—and I'm chaperoning his class field trip this morning."

And thankfully, Callie thought, if the sound of multiple chain saws echoing in the distance was any indication, Nash Echols was very busy, too.

NASH HADN'T FIGURED Callie could look any lovelier than she had the previous night. But when she opened the door this evening, she proved him wrong yet again. In a white sweater set and black plaid skirt, her hair falling loosely around her face, she was a picture of maternal beauty.

Callie also didn't seem all that surprised to see him, though he had given her no warning for fear she'd tell him not to drop by.

He held up the reason for his visit. "Here's the info you wanted."

"Mommy!" Brian shouted from inside the house. "Mommy! Need you!"

Without warning, her son came dashing around the corner and into the hall that ran the length of the stairs, and into the foyer. "My friend!" Brian said, in surprise. Hands spread wide and high in the air, he ran toward Nash and catapulted into his arms.

Nash caught him and lifted him high in the air. 'Well, what do you know—" he winked and was rewarded with a burst of giggles "—it is *my* friend, Hortense!"

"Brian," Callie's son corrected.

Nash made a face. "Jimmy-Bob?" He tried again with comic intent.

More giggles. "No." Brian held up his arms. "*Brian!*"

"Oh." Nash reacted as if he'd had an epiphany. "Brian!"

"Yes."

"Well, how are you, friend?" Nash asked.

"Make candy. House," Brian said, squirming in his arms. When Nash gently set him down so the little boy could run off again, Brian tugged at Nash's hand. "Come see."

Nash looked at Callie, a question mark in his eyes.

"Sure," she said, after a small pause. She flashed a faint welcoming smile that was probably more good manners than any sincere wish to spend time with him.

It was better than the greeting he'd expected, however.

So Nash grinned back and let her assume he thought she was as genuinely happy to see him as he was to see her.

"Wow," he remarked when they rounded the corner into the kitchen. Thick white frosting and layers of gingerbread covered the cardboard bungalow he and Callie had built the night before. On top of that was more frosting and a smattering of gumdrops and assorted other candy that had clearly been placed by a child.

Nash pulled up a chair and sank into it backward. He rested his hands along the rungs and took a moment to admire the colorful decoration. "Did you do all this?"

"Mommy help," Brian said proudly.

"We've been 'done' for a while now, at least for this evening," Callie interjected, "but I've been unable to convince my culinary assistant that it is time to hang up our aprons and call it a night."

Nash grinned at the way she was talking in code to ward off a temper tantrum.

"Perhaps you could do the honors?" She looked at him.

"Hey, bud, isn't it time you got in your pajamas."

"No." Brian said stubbornly. He picked up a green gumdrop and pressed it onto the top of a red one, already glued to the roofline. With no frosting there, it fell off.

The lower lip went out.

Uh-oh, Nash thought.

Callie picked up the spoon with icing on the back of it. "Here," she said to her son. "Let's put a little frosting on the back of it and…"

"No," Brian pouted. He held the green gumdrop out of Callie's reach, moved around and tried to stick it on a purple gumdrop. Without frosting, it fell to the table again.

Callie reached for it. Brian got to it first. "*Me do it!*" he yelled in frustration.

"Honey, it won't..."

Glowering, Brian let out a rebel yell and pressed the gumdrop as hard as he could into the middle of the roof.

A dent appeared where none had been, and the gingerbread began to crumble.

Brian stomped his foot and began to sob.

Nash picked the little boy up into his arms and carried him across to the not yet decorated tree. "Hey now, buddy," he said. "That happens to all of us and it's nothing that can't be fixed."

Brian cried all the harder.

Callie disappeared for several long moments, but Nash kept talking, soothing as best he could. When she returned, she had a baby blanket and a stuffed pink pig in her arms. She held her arms out to a still sobbing Brian. This time he went willingly.

Before Nash knew it, they were moving upstairs, and he was alone again. Not about to leave until he was sure she didn't need his help putting Brian to bed, he ambled back over to the table and sat down in front of it.

In the distance, the squalling waned, then stopped entirely. Five minutes later, she was back. "You fixed the roof!" she said, looking both exhausted and relieved.

He put down the spoon he'd been using to smooth the edges. "Didn't I tell you? I was a pastry chef in a former life?"

Looking more frazzled than ever, Callie blinked. "Really?"

"Nah. But this frosting is sort of like glue, as I'm sure you know, and if you slather enough of it on, you can apparently fix just about anything."

Callie drew up a chair and sank into it. "Sorry about his behavior."

Nash shrugged, glad to have things going back to semi-normal. "He's two and a half. I think that's how they're supposed to act." He teased her with a wink. "Especially when it gets close to their bedtime."

A delicate flush crept across her cheeks. "Or past it, in Brian's case." She looked at Nash and sighed. "He was pretty wound up from his field trip today."

Nash nodded, knowing he should go. Wanting to stay. So he lingered as she got up again and went to the stove, put the teakettle on. "Yeah, I heard about that."

Callie tensed. For a moment, she didn't move. "From whom?"

"Hart." Nash waited until she turned to face him again, before he continued, "He stopped by to pick up a few trees for some people in his office. I guess Maggie had filled him in." Unable to resist, Nash grinned and asked, "So how many guys did he identify as his potential daddy?"

CALLIE SHOULD HAVE known a cutup like Nash would bring this up. She covered her face with her hands, still reeling with remembered humiliation. "Three firemen and two policemen. He got a laugh every time, so you can imagine how eager he was to try it again."

Nash stood and hovered closer. "Pretty eager, I'm guessing."

Callie got out two packets of instant spiced apple cider. "Very eager, as it happens."

She ripped both open and shook them into mugs. Looked like he was staying on, at least for a little bit. He watched her as she walked past him to throw the empty packets in the trash. Damn, she smelled good, too. Like gingerbread and sugar, and the special fragrance that was just…Callie.

She peered at him again, this time beneath a fringe of thick dark lashes. As if thinking about throwing him out—before they could even think about flirting or kissing again…

He sobered. "Do you know you have frosting in your hair?"

"Noooooo." Her eyes glittered as if she weren't sure if he was joking or not.

He wasn't.

She lifted a hand to the left. He pointed to the right. She ran her palm over her curls and still missed it. So he stepped forward and ever so gently removed the sticky substance clumped in the strand. Then he opened his palm so she could see what her decorating had wrought. "Hmm."

"What? No thanks?"

"Okay," she said drolly. "Thanks."

"You're welcome. And by the way," he continued, as the teakettle began to whistle, "how come you have no rings on your left hand?"

Maggie switched off the burner and grabbed the kettle. Once again, she managed not to look at him as she filled the mugs. "It's because I'm having an allergic re-action." She stirred the contents of each mug briskly, then handed him his.

"An allergic reaction," he repeated, being careful to hold the stoneware by the handle.

She remained lounging against the counter, some distance away. "Yes. An allergic reaction."

"To me?" He studied her over the rim of the mug. "Or to continuing to pretend to be married?"

"Verrrry funny."

Nash had thought so.

Callie paused. "Turns out there might be something on the rings or in the setting that is causing said allergic reaction."

"Really?"

"Yes." She released a breath. "So when I asked my parents for their medical advice, they told me to take my rings to the jeweler's to be professionally cleaned, and to also have the setting checked."

"And?"

"The jewelry store is pretty busy this time of year, so the rings won't be ready to be picked up for another week or so."

Nash tried not to feel relieved about that. Although he was pretty sure everyone who cared about Callie knew that the longer she was away from those rings, and the now defunct marriage they represented, the better. "So how is your hand today?"

"I don't know." Callie set down her mug and held out her hand. "I haven't looked at it since I put the moisture-proof bandages on this morning. But now that you mention it, it is feeling a little itchy."

He set his mug down, too. "I could unwrap it for you.'

A lift of her chin. "Is that the only thing you want to unwrap?"

He moved his brows playfully. "What do *you* think?"

She held up both hands in a gesture that seemed both warning—and surrender. Then slayed him with a look that invited him to do what no one had been able to accomplish thus far—to try to tear down the barriers around her heart, to find the emotionally vulnerable woman underneath. "Nash…" Her tone was soft. Wary. Enticing.

He caught her palm and held it over his thudding heart. "Just a kiss, Callie. To hold us over."

She caught her breath at the sensual intent in his gaze, and went very still. Her delicate brows arched inquisitively. "Until what?"

Nash lowered his head, tilting it slightly to one side, so his lips were just above hers. He threaded his hands through her silky ringlets. "The next time we make love."

Her lips fell apart in surprise. He moved in to kiss her, intending only to curb their frustration and restore humor to a situation that was fast getting out of control. She swayed against him for a millisecond. Satisfaction roared through him. Then her hand came up, pushed on the center of his chest.

She squared her shoulders and drew back, with customary resolve—and maybe a bit of sass, too. "I've got a better idea."

Sounded good. Especially if it meant they were about to head upstairs again…

Aqua-blue eyes sparkling with a light he couldn't quite decipher but was enamored of anyhow, she took his hand and led him toward the hallway that ran from the front of the house to the back. "Come with me…"

Anytime.

Only instead of heading upstairs—to her bedroom—she stopped at the door tucked under the stairs. "Since you're so tall…"

He did have a good seven inches on her…

"And such a manly man…"

Okay, he wasn't sure if she was serious about that accolade or not.

She let go of his hand, opened the door and reached for a red-and-green plastic storage container. "How about you do us both a favor?" The corners of her lips curved mischievously. "And help me finish something that absolutely must be done?"

Chapter Eight

Nash stared at Callie, as if unable to comprehend the task. Which, given what he had clearly expected her to ask him to do, was understandable. "You want me to carry storage boxes for you?" he repeated.

"For starters," Callie admitted, pulling out three for him and keeping three for herself. Pretending he wasn't her greatest male fantasy come to life, she shut the closet door with her hip. "All of them need to be taken into the family room. Then I'm hoping you'll volunteer to help string lights on the tree."

He fell into line behind her. "I think it's pretty clear by now I'll follow you anywhere."

Trying not to think of the view she had just inadvertently given him, she turned and arched a brow. "Really, Echols. Still flirting?"

He grinned at her deadpan tone, then responded in kind. "Let's just say you bring out the 'manly man' in me."

Callie couldn't help it—she laughed. If there was ever a guy with too much testosterone...

As if on cue, he set the boxes down and folded his arms across his brawny chest.

Callie swallowed hard. She told herself not to stare, to

keep things light and carefree, but it was difficult with him showcasing all those magnificently sculpted muscles right in front of her.

"So is your tree decorated?" she asked, forcing her attention back to the conversation.

Broad shoulders flexed.

"Tell me you even *have* a tree."

Another somewhat evasive smile. "The guys got me one already."

She trod closer. Studying him, she inclined her head. "Why do I feel there's a catch to that?"

His sexy grin widened while he contemplated that. He rubbed the flat of his hand across the bottom of his jaw. "Let's just say it has a lot of personality."

Uh-huh. "Where is it?" she asked.

"Currently?" His expression was one of total innocence. "Standing in a bucket of water on my back porch."

He was kidding. Wait…he *wasn't* kidding. "Echols!" she chided, upset. Even she, with her problem celebrating Christmas in her heart, knew that was no way to treat a holiday tree.

He ambled closer, too, not stopping until there were mere inches between them. "You know I like it when you call me by last name. It's sort of a turn-on."

Figuring the best way to avoid making out with him again was to get busy again, Callie lifted the lid off a box and pulled out a long strand of white Christmas lights. "Now that I know that," she said dryly, "I'll be sure and go back to Nash."

Callie unraveled one end and handed it to him. He held on to it while she kept right on unraveling. "Back to your tree," she continued. "Why is it on your back porch?"

Another mysterious shrug. "I haven't had a chance to bring it in."

"And if I buy that, I'm sure you have some mountain air you'd like to sell me…"

Now that they'd completely unwound the strand, he strolled over to plug it in. The test worked. The lights all came on.

"Nor do I actually have any decorations." He wandered back to the tree and, accepting her wordless direction, began threading the lights through the top of the pine.

"What about your uncle?" Once again, Callie tried not to notice how his soft flannel shirt stretched across the taut muscles of his chest.

Nash paused, treading more carefully now. "If he had any, I can't figure out where he would have put them, except the attic, which is a pretty jumbled mess. For all I know, he never even bothered putting up a tree himself."

Like uncle, like nephew.

Sensing there was something behind that sudden faint glimmer of sadness and outward cool, Callie asked, even more casually, "You never visited your uncle at Christmastime?" From what she had come to understand, Nash and his folks were all the relatives Ralph Echols had.

Nash moved around behind the tree, focused on his task. "No. Just summers mostly. When we—I," he corrected with a shake of his head, "was out of school and had the time to come and stay awhile." So his parents hadn't visited then, either, Callie deduced, following Nash around the tree.

Silence fell between them as he bent to thread the lights through the branches at midtree.

"What did you do in the summers?" he asked finally.

Callie reflected with a smile and a small shrug. "Survived the chaos, mostly."

He lifted a speculative brow. "Care to elaborate…"

Trying not to think what his low, masculine voice did to rev up her insides, Callie took a trip down memory lane. "Well… My oldest sister, Poppy, was always painting and rearranging and redecorating stuff. My twin, Maggie—whom you now know—and I both babysat a lot. The *triplets* loved spending time at the pool. Lily was on the swim team. Rose worked in the snack bar. And Violet lifeguarded."

Nash blinked. "Your parents had *triplets*—in addition to *twins*?" Briefly, he looked terrified by the notion of all those children and all that estrogen. Which was, Callie admitted wryly, the usual reaction to the knowledge she had five sisters. Five of whom were multiples!

Callie lifted a hand, reminding, "And don't forget Poppy—the only single birth. She gets ticked off whenever she's discounted." Boy, did she get ticked off.

Which made sense. Callie knew it couldn't have been fun to be the regular-birthed kid amidst all that chaos and excitement.

"I guess Poppy would at that." He paused, recollecting. "They all had flower names…?"

"Including me, since my given name is Calla. I just like going by Callie."

He remained flabbergasted. "Wow."

Finished with one strand of lights, Callie went to get the other. "So does this mean you now want to meet all my sisters?"

Nash took the end and they began the same unraveling process. "Depends." He slanted her a wicked look. "Are they all as gorgeous and funny and sexy as you?"

"Subtle," she replied with a grin. "And not at all."

They laughed together, then kept working. The second strand went faster. Once they were finally done, Callie plugged the end into a power strip, then handed Nash a tree-topper in the shape of a star. He plugged that into the existing strands. And suddenly it was all lit up. Ready for her son to help her decorate the next day.

Callie stepped back to admire their handiwork, acutely aware just how much she enjoyed spending time with Nash—no matter what they were doing. She propped her hands on her hips, conscious of the fact that her attempt at staying busy had failed. She still wanted to pull him close and make out with him. More than he would ever know.

She forced her attention away from her fantasies and back to the task at hand. "Hey, that really looks nice. Thanks for helping me out with it."

He winked. "Anytime you need a manly man, you just call. I'll come running, promise."

CALLIE KNEW NASH WOULD, which was precisely the problem. She had to get some boundaries erected between them, and fast. And the best way she knew to do that was to forget the personal, yet again, and concentrate strictly on the business.

She squared her shoulders and went to get her work calendar. "Before I forget, there are a few things I should mention."

Clearly intrigued, he met her gaze. "Okay."

"My in-laws are going to be here on Thursday evening."

His brow furrowed. "Meaning what? You want me to make myself scarce?"

"Of course you can come over on a purely professional basis."

"But," he concluded, smile fading, "you'd just rather I not drop in."

His sardonic tone stung. Callie pressed her lips together, tried again. "Doris and Rock tend to...overreact... to things." Which was putting it mildly.

"Like when they said you were going to have the best corporate retreat in all of Texas, right out of the gate."

"They mean well. But...it's a lot of pressure to put on a person, if you know what I mean."

He nodded, beginning to understand. "You think they'd disapprove of our friendship," he said quietly.

Callie walked Nash into the hall and handed him his coat. "I'm not really sure how they would feel." She paused to look into his eyes. "And given how much I have on my plate, I'd rather not find out just now."

His expression gentled. "Understood."

"Thanks."

Nash pulled on his coat and headed toward the door. "How long are they staying?"

"Through Saturday afternoon. They're going to help out with Brian while I host my second executive retreat on Friday, and then attend the organizational meeting for the Old-Fashioned Christmas Celebration at the Double Knot Ranch."

"The Grimes are participating in that, too?" he asked in surprise.

"Doris and Rock won't be working the actual event— they have a conflict on that date. But their company is going to be supplying some of the Texana memorabilia we're going to be putting in the gift baskets. So they will be there Saturday, taking orders and nailing down the details of the giveaways. As a participant, you should be at the organizational meeting, too." She paused, aware this should have been mentioned sooner. "Will that be a problem?"

He shook his head. "My last day to cut down trees is on Thursday. The trucking company will pick them all up on Friday."

She walked with him onto the front porch. The night was clear and cold and filled with the smell of wood smoke and pine. "And then what?" she asked, suddenly reluctant to see her time with him end.

Oblivious to the romantic nature of her thoughts, he said, "I begin cataloging trees and making a list of the native shrubs I'll excavate and the big pines I plan to cut down next spring. But that's a ways off."

Callie nodded, as if she hadn't just been thinking of kissing him again. "So you'll have plenty of time to help out with the preparations for the holiday celebration?" she said in her most businesslike tone.

Nash turned his collar up against the chill and headed briskly down the steps. "Anything you want," he called over his shoulder. "You just let me know…"

SINCE HE HAD been warned to steer clear of Doris and Rock Grimes, Nash was more than a little surprised to see Doris drive up to his ranch Friday afternoon. He handed out the last of the paychecks to the departing horse and cattle wranglers turned temporary lumber-jacks, then walked over to greet Callie's former mother-in-law. She was dressed as eclectically as ever and had an unusually serious expression on her face.

Aware Callie had an event going on next door, Nash asked, "Everything okay?"

Doris nodded. "Mind if I talk to you for a few minutes?"

"Would you like to go inside?"

Doris looked around at the blue sky and unseasonably warm December afternoon, taking in the abrupt but not unusual change in the Texas weather. "It's so beautiful here on the mountain. How about we sit on the porch?"

Nash escorted her to an Adirondack chair. "So what's on your mind?"

Doris wrapped her lightweight shawl around her. "Callie, obviously. And Brian. Rock and I are worried about them."

"In what sense?"

"The holidays have always been hard for Callie since my son died," she explained. "And now with Brian becoming a handful at times as well, Rock and I would feel better if we knew her closest neighbor was keeping an eye on her."

Nash heard the caution in her tone, and felt it, too. "What about Fiona and Frank Sanders—on her other side?" Wouldn't they have been the logical first choice?

"Her sister, Maggie's, in-laws? They're already watching out for Callie and Brian, but they are also awfully busy at the Double Knot Wedding Ranch. And since you're obviously spending a lot of time over at her place now, at least according to Brian…"

"He's mentioned me?"

Another nod. "He seems to think you are the leading candidate for becoming his new daddy." Doris surveyed him carefully, waiting for Nash's reaction.

Doing his best to maintain a poker face, he lifted a hand. "I understand Brian's confused about that storybook of his…and how it might apply to his own life."

Another long, steady look. "He also likes you very much."

"I like him, too," Nash said sincerely. But that did not mean he and Callie were getting married. Especially since she had said more than once that she was dead set against ever tying the knot again. Past romantic experience told him if he were wise, he would take her word on that. Not push for more.

Doris handed him a business card. "Because you're nearby and might be the first to notice if there is anything amiss, Rock and I would appreciate it if you would let us know if Callie and or Brian need anything. We travel constantly for our business, but all our contact information is on the card."

Nash paused. "You're that worried about her?"

Doris hesitated, then finally said, "Really, it's just a precaution."

Then why, Nash wondered, did he get the feeling that it was a helluva lot more than that?

"GOT A MINUTE to talk privately?" Nash asked Hart later the same day.

"Sure." His friend led him into his office at Sanders Security Services. He shut the door behind them and gestured for Nash to have a seat. "What's up?"

"I had a visit from Callie's former mother-in-law this afternoon." Briefly, Nash recounted the conversation. "Do you have any idea what's behind her request?"

Abruptly, Hart looked as if he were about to walk over hot coals. "Callie can't know I told you any of this."

"Okay."

He settled behind his desk. "She came here to have a fresh start."

Nash sat down, too. "What happened?"

Hart picked up a pen and turned it end-over-end. "You know her husband died right before the holidays a few months after she was married, right?"

"Yeah…but I don't really know much more than that."

"Callie was a couple of months pregnant at the time," Hart began. "At first, she seemed to take it remarkably well. According to Maggie, she cried and stuff, but she seemed to soldier on. Stayed in Dallas. Kept working her job. Had as normal a life as possible."

This was beginning to sound ominous. "And then what happened?"

His friend grimaced. "She was at a big Christmas party for her job at some swanky downtown Dallas hotel. And she just lost it. Started crying. Couldn't stop. They had to hospitalize her for exhaustion. Her parents had to come and take her back to Laramie. They got her into counseling. She joined a grief group. Had the baby."

Nash paused to take all that in. Although he knew she was a passionate woman at heart, it was hard to imagine Callie as anything but strong and resolute. "And was okay after that?" Nash guessed, still feeling a little rattled by the revelation.

"Till the next Christmas. Then the same thing happened. Not as bad. I mean, she wasn't out in public or anything, but again—according to Maggie—she had a pretty bad couple of days."

"How old was Brian then?"

"Six months, I think. Anyway, Callie recovered pretty quickly from that relapse, and she went on with her life, but the word was out she was still struggling to cope with the loss of her husband and she got a lot of sympathy, which she interpreted as pity. You know the drill from your own experiences."

Nash's gut tightened. "Yeah. Grief sucks. And it's even worse when everyone is watching you, ready to rush in at the smallest sign you might not be as 'over it' at that moment as everyone wants you to be."

Hart sympathized, too.

Nash rested his arms on the sides of his chair. "How was she the second year after her husband's death?"

"There was a day or two before the holidays when she had an anniversary reaction, but she talked to her counselor and seemed to come even more to terms with her loss." He cleared his throat. "Especially when she made the decision to start fresh and create a whole new life for herself, first by taking a position with my parents in their business, and then by using Seth's life insurance money to buy her own ranch and start her own company."

"And the third year?"

"Nothing of note this year, thus far," Hart said inconsequentially. "Unless you've noticed something…?"

Aside from a rash on her ring finger and an apparently uncharacteristic desire to have a fling with him? "I wouldn't know what to look for."

"You understand grief."

Better than anyone. How it hit when you least expected it, and that the only thing that really helped was time. And a willingness to recover.

Aware his old friend was still sizing him up, Nash shrugged. "Yeah, but I don't have a good handle on Callie." One minute he thought he understood her, and the next…

Nash thought about the fact he might be dealing with a ticking emotional time bomb. He exhaled roughly. "What do you think all this means? How do you think your sister-in-law is doing?"

Hart lifted a hand. "She's either far enough along in her grief process to be able to accept the death of her husband and not suffer the way she did in past holiday seasons…"

"Or the worst is yet to come," Nash surmised unhappily.

Hart lowered his brow. "For the record, I think she's ready to move on. She's certainly been happier the past few weeks than I recall seeing her in a very long time."

Nash hoped her willingness to get involved with him—even on a strictly physical level thus far—proved that was indeed the case. That if her mind and body were moving on, soon her heart would be, too. Because if there was anything he knew for certain, it was that a woman as spirited and beautiful as Callie was not destined to end up alone.

Curious, he asked, "Is that why her parents didn't want her to leave Laramie and move here?"

Hart nodded. "Jackson and Lacey McCabe worry Callie might be too isolated at the ranch. Seth's parents feel the same way."

"And yet," Nash noted, "Doris and Rock Grimes apparently support Callie's decision to strike out on her own, away from Laramie."

"Probably because they worry if Callie were to stay in Laramie, she would always be viewed as Seth's widow. And they really want her to marry again. They want their grandson to grow up with a mother and a father in his life." Hart studied Nash. "Is this going to be hard for you?"

Of course his old friend would ask. And of course he

would dodge the question in return. "Why would it be?" he challenged mildly.

Another long, telling look. "The similarities."

"Callie is nothing like my parents," Nash declared flatly.

Because if she were, he could not be involved with her. It was as simple—and heartbreakingly difficult—as that.

To Nash's relief, though, Callie seemed more together than ever when he saw her the next day at the Double Knot Ranch party barn. "You're in a chipper mood," he observed as she stepped up to take his measurements for the costumes that everyone working the event would be wearing.

"With good reason." Callie ran the measuring tape from his shoulder to wrist. "Seven hundred and fifty-two people of the one thousand we invited have RSVP'd that they will be attending the first annual Old-Fashioned Christmas Celebration. Plus…" Callie paused to scribble down a number, then moved in to wrap the tape around his waist "…the event at my ranch on Friday was a wild success, with the group so pleased they have already booked three more events. One each quarter, for the next year. With the possibility of an even bigger Christmas bash next year."

"That is good news."

"Plus, Brian and I have had a nice visit with my in-laws."

Nash looked over to see her little boy walking around with his grandfather, hand in hand. "And as you can clearly see, my son has calmed down somewhat from where he was earlier in the week." Callie wrote down a second number, stepped back. "Why are you looking at me funny?"

Nash pushed aside his earlier worry and shrugged. "No reason. Nice to see you so happy, is all."

Callie laughed. "'Tis the spirit of the season," she said lightly. "But you're right." She paused reflectively, her blue eyes sparkling. "I haven't felt this genuinely festive in a long time."

He leaned forward to whisper conspiratorially, "Like you almost have the real Christmas spirit?"

Tensing only slightly, she whispered back, "I wouldn't go that far. But—" she looked around again to make sure no one was listening "—I was going to take Brian to get some pizza and see the light displays in San Antonio this evening." She knelt to get his inseam, the sight of her before him like that almost enough to make him groan.

Clearly having no idea at all what was on his mind, she asked, "Interested in tagging along with us?"

With effort, Nash ignored the feel of her hands brushing against his inseam. "You bet."

To Callie's delight, her son remained the perfect little angel even after he said goodbye to his grandparents. His exemplary behavior continued throughout dinner with Nash, and then the drive to see the lights.

Nash was on his best behavior, too.

Actually, he appeared a little on the cautious side. Studying her kindly one minute, treating her with reverent tenderness the next.

And that irritated—and confused—her.

She liked the way he challenged her. Made her defend her actions as well as her feelings and come out of her self-imposed safety zone to deal with him head-on. Now, suddenly, instead of going toe-to-toe with her, the way he had from the first moment they had crossed paths, he was starting to treat her with kid gloves.

Why, she didn't know.

Unless it was guilt. Because he thought he had seduced her unfairly. When really it was the other way around...

She figured she would find out later. Or be forever distracted by the shift in his attitude from sexy devilry to the perfect Texas gentleman.

In the meantime, she knew, there was still much to revel in.

So she sat back in the luxurious leather passenger seat of Nash's pickup truck and focused on enjoying the festive sights along with her son and the handsome man beside her.

"Look, Mommy! Santa! Reindeer! Angel, Mommy. Snowman!"

And so it went.

Brian identified everything he saw with shouts of joy. By the time they got back home, carrying their boxed-up leftover pizza, he was fast asleep in his car seat.

Still fretting a little over Nash's quiet mood, Callie unlocked the door while he carried her little boy inside and right up to his bed. Brian didn't wake while she put him in his pajamas. A good sign he was out for the night.

Callie went back downstairs. Nash was standing in front of the fireplace, hands shoved in the back pockets of his jeans, his jacket still on. He turned to her, every bit the gentleman she had wanted him to be from the outset.

Only tonight, Callie realized, it wasn't his good manners she was interested in. She walked toward him, suddenly not wanting him to leave. On impulse, she kissed his cheek, found her way to his mouth. "Thank you for tonight." She hugged him fiercely. "You were great."

He turned toward her so they had full-body contact. "So were you." Threading his hands through her hair, he bent his head and kissed her again. Slowly and deliberately. Until her mind was rife with all the possibilities she'd been forcing herself not to consider. She wanted a relationship again.

With him.

How crazy was that?

His eyes opened, smoldering and intense. He studied her as if he found her as endlessly fascinating as she found him. Lower still, his hardness pressed against her. And yet, to her mounting frustration, he was still treating her like some fragile flower. Which was the last thing she wanted. *Especially* from him.

"Something on your mind?" she asked finally, easing him out of his coat. Which wasn't easy, since he half resisted her on that, too.

"Yeah." The word was rough, impatient, in the way his touch was still not. "What is this?"

When she tried to evade his dark, penetrating look, he eased her back against the wall. Her heart pounded as he framed her face with his hands. And something unfurled deep inside her.

"Um…sex?" The beginning of what she hoped would be *more sex*?

Nash scowled at her lame attempt at a joke. "You know what I mean," he said impatiently, giving her another long, indeterminable look. "Is this something fun and easy?"

Or in other words, the kind of thing that could end

up breaking her heart—if she ever let her heart get in-volved?

"An actual date?" He continued his litany of choices with a certain unexpected weariness of soul. "The beginning of another one-night stand?"

Which, clearly, Callie noted by his deepening frown, wasn't good with him.

He prodded her with a lift of his dark brow. "Something more?" he asked, the weariness sliding into hope. "Like the beginning of a long-term affair?"

Unable to bear the way he was searching her face, never mind the long-suppressed emotions he was conjuring up, Callie made a frustrated sound. Sighed.

He brought her close and kissed her again, even more persuasively. Until her breasts pearled and her knees weakened. Then he made his way down her throat.

Still a force of masculinity and stubborn resolve, he continued to persist.

"Or something a lot less…?"

It sure felt like a *lot*.

Except not less…more.

So much so, it felt like she was on the brink of falling in love.

But not wanting to say that out loud for fear of exposing herself to heartbreak again, she shook her head, looked deep into his eyes and coaxed a smile from him instead.

For reasons she told herself she was just going to have to accept, Nash seemed to be wanting reassurance that she would be okay no matter how this attraction of theirs turned out.

And now that she finally knew how strong she was,

that was something, Callie realized, she could actually give him.

"I don't know what this is, Nash." Her back still against the wall, she reached up and kissed him in return. Reveling in the hot, male taste of him, she admitted, "I'm doing my best to try to figure it out. In the meantime, I'm not about to confuse sex and love. And…" Callie flattened herself against him, ready to let herself need—to feel—just a little bit. "Neither should you."

His body relaxed in relief. "Sure?"

"Positive." Determined to prove she spoke the truth, Callie molded her mouth to his, savoring his heat and strength, the fact he was so big and tall and male. So upfront about his desire for her. Yet so willing, when he let his guard down, too, to let her call the shots and set the pace, if that was what she wanted.

She sighed, inhaling the brisk, wintry scent of his cologne, the unique masculine fragrance of his skin. Then set about to show him how truly unfragile she was. And got his deep, steady pursuit, his ability to make her practically burst into flames with just a kiss, instead.

She didn't know why she was so surprised he had taken what she started and commandeered this for his own. When Nash put his mind to something, he persevered with single-minded concentration. And when he wanted to tease her to distraction, and maybe start to seduce her in the process, well, he did that, too.

Excited to have him finally reacting the way she wanted him to, she fisted her hands in his shirt and rose on tiptoe, aware that once again she was incredibly, amazingly alive.

As was he…

Dear Lord, so was he.

His mouth continued working little miracles, first on her lips, then her jaw, down her throat, to the *U* of her collarbone. She shuddered against him, wanting him desperately, trembling with need. Then he kissed her again, until he was breathing as raggedly as she was.

He slipped a hand beneath the hem of her sweater, past her bra, to the top curve of her breast. Her body melted into the possessive caress.

He drew back to look at her. Smiling now. Definitely reassured. "Figured it out yet?"

She grinned at the return of his playful side. "Figured what out?"

He found her nipple, caressing it so gently she moaned.

"What this is."

"Still working on it," she promised, kissing him again, and jumping back into life.

"Me, too," he murmured back, sounding every bit as intent on finding intense satisfaction as she was.

Callie laughed. "That and more," she said coyly.

Bodies on fire from the inside out, still making out, they slow-danced their way through the living room, up the stairs, down the hall, to her bedroom. Behind the locked door, in the soft lamplight of her bedroom, they faced each other yet again.

And Callie knew.

None of this was simple, not at all. But at least she had one thing.

Somewhere in the past fifteen minutes, Nash had stopped treating her with kid gloves.

NASH LET HER tug her sweater over her head just because it was so exciting to watch her begin a deliberate striptease. He took over when it came to her bra. Her breasts were round and luscious, the nipples a deep impertinent rose. He bent his head, resolved to cherish and care for her the way she deserved. She tasted every bit as good as he recalled, and he moaned, taking her all the way into his mouth. She quivered against him, holding him close, urging him on.

Heart racing, he found the zipper to her jeans. When they were both naked yet again, he backed her toward the bed. He kissed her long and hard and deep, until she made that helpless sound, low and soft, in the back of her throat, the sound that said she knew how much he wanted her and always would, and his own blood began to boil.

Determined to make her his, he knelt before her, positioning himself between her legs, stroking the silken insides of her thighs and the satiny petals until dampness flowed. Over and over, his fingers made lazy circles, moved up, in, his lips hotly, rapaciously tracing the sensual trail. She arched, bucked, suddenly right where he wanted her, shuddering with release, pleading, murmuring his name.

Eager to please her even more, he drew her down onto the bed.

"My turn," she rasped, moving over him. Giving him everything he wanted, her fingers, hands, lips roving over him, laying claim to every sensitive ridge and plane.

Taking his time, making it last, he lifted her over the top of him. Straddling him, she gave him full rein, her back arching as he slowly, deliberately penetrated her, her thighs falling even farther apart.

Until he was aware of every soft, warm inch of her, inside and out. Every sigh of surrender and pulsation of need. Until there was no more reason, no more holding back, nothing but pleasure for both of them. Only a sweet, swirling oblivion that led to the most magnificent peace Nash had ever known.

For long moments, they held each other tightly, still shuddering, breathing hard.

This time, when she collapsed against him, her face pressed against his neck, she didn't pull away. Loving the warmth and softness of her, he stroked one hand through her hair, cuddled her closer still.

Finally he lifted his head and, unable to resist, said, "Just out of curiosity…*is this* a date?"

She laughed, as he meant her to. And continued looking at him as if she, too, felt connected in a very fundamental way.

"Not sure about that, either," she drawled, looking every bit as strong and resolute as he had estimated her to be.

Gently, she rubbed her palm across his chest. "What do *you* think?" Her hand came to rest in the region of his heart. Her gaze grew as tender as her voice. She waited for his response.

"It's definitely something," he proclaimed tenderly. And to prove it, he rolled so she was beneath him, and made love to her all over again, even more slowly and thoroughly this time.

ALTHOUGH CALLIE WAS tempted to stay wrapped in Nash's arms and fall asleep, she knew it would be too confusing for her son to find *his friend Nash* there in the morning.

And maybe, despite the depth and breadth of her attraction to Nash, too unsettling for her, too. Because although she knew she was ripe for "just an affair"— and a possibly short-lived one at that, given how confused things still were—she wasn't sure Nash was. So as soon as her aftershocks faded, she extricated herself from his arms, rose, slipped on a robe and went to check on her son.

To her relief, Brian was sleeping soundly.

Restless, she went back downstairs, where the lights were still blazing. Realizing she was starving, she found her way into the kitchen.

Seconds later, Nash joined her. Barefoot, jeans on and unsnapped, unbuttoned shirt hanging loosely across his broad shoulders, he looked sexy, disheveled and tender as could be.

Her heart took a telltale leap, then constricted with the equally potent fear that she was getting in too fast, too deep.

"Missed you."

"Couldn't sleep," she fibbed.

He ambled closer, wrapped a possessive arm about her waist and pressed a kiss on the top of her head. "Without you, neither could I." He looked around and saw she was already preheating the oven. "So. What's going on?"

"I'm hungry. How about you?"

He nodded. Waited. As if knowing there was a lot on her mind.

Callie sighed. "I thought I would feel guilty when I finally made love with someone again." She layered the leftover pizza on a baking sheet and slid it in the oven. Going to the fridge, she brought out a couple of Texas beers and two slices of lime. Maybe it was time to relax.

He accepted the drink with a wordless look of thanks. "And did you?"

"A little." Callie paused to work the citrus wedge into

the neck of the bottle. "The first time." She'd also been pretty confused.

He untwisted the cap on his and took a sip of the golden brew. "And now?"

Callie drew a breath and said honestly, "To my surprise, I'm not at all conflicted." She felt, as odd as it might sound, that the two of them were fated to be together.

"And that bothers you?"

Callie took another sip of the simultaneously tart and mellow beverage. "A little. I never thought I was the type of person to have a casual affair, or to make love without being in love, but…"

Setting his beer aside, he hooked his foot beneath the rung of the chair, sank down into it and pulled her onto his lap. His hands moved soothingly up and down her spine. "Keep talking."

Callie settled cozily on his thighs and wreathed her arms around his strong, warm shoulders. "I really like being with you." She smiled affectionately. "And Brian enjoys your company, as well."

He lifted the curtain of her hair, brushing against her chin, and kissed the shell of her ear. "I really like being with you and your son, too."

Callie swallowed, as she began to feel nervous all over again. She arched her brow. "Sensing a pattern here?"

His gaze narrowed. "If so, it's definitely one I like." He hugged her close before drawing back again to lock gazes with her. "We don't have to put a label on this, Callie." Gently, he tucked her hair behind her ear. "We don't have to think about what it all means, at least not right now."

Her anxiety beginning to subside, Callie studied him

in return. "You're okay with that?" she asked. "Taking it one day, one moment, at a time?"

Nash nodded. He tilted his head and kissed her again, even more tenderly and evocatively. "I am."

Chapter Nine

Nash opened the door Sunday afternoon to a very welcome sight. Brian stood next to his mother, a yellow kiddie construction hat tilting precariously on his dark head. A tool belt was slung around his waist. He held a toy wrench in one hand, a play screwdriver in the other.

"Ho, ho, ho, and Merry Christmas!" Callie exclaimed, a bag of goodies in each hand. "We're here to help you put up your tree!"

"Me fix." Brian held up a screwdriver and wrench. He could not have been more serious.

"Long story." Callie shook her head, her chocolate-brown curls bouncing around her face. "Involving a very convoluted misunderstanding that doesn't bear going into. Suffice it to say, this little elf got the idea that your tree needed fixing, and fixing usually involves tools of some sort. And, well, you can see the rest for yourself."

"Actually, little Brian here is not far off the mark," Nash admitted, happily ushering them in.

She blinked. "What do you mean?"

With a wink, he walked them through the house and out the back door, to the bucket on the back porch. "I'll let you decide for yourself."

Callie stopped at what she saw. "That's…"

Aware how pretty she looked, standing there in the afternoon light, Nash couldn't help but chuckle. "The saddest little tree you've ever seen in your life?"

She whirled to face him in a drift of hyacinth perfume. "Well, it does give new meaning to the phrase a Charlie Brown Christmas Tree."

"Beginning to see why I didn't rush to put it up?"

"Um…yeah…actually…" With a slant of her head, she conceded him the point.

Oblivious to their disdain, Brian pointed to the tree, then the top of his own head. "Look, Mommy. Me."

Callie interpreted for Nash. "I think he's trying to say it's his height."

"It is indeed," he observed. "At least on the one side that has branches."

Callie moved around to see what he meant. "Oh! It is a little lopsided, isn't it?"

Exactly why it had made such a good prank.

She sauntered back to his side, standing comfortably close. "How come you haven't gotten rid of it?"

He shrugged. "I felt a little sorry for it, to tell the truth."

"I see…" Callie wavered, as if not sure what to do next.

Nash figured, however, that it was not too soon for Brian to learn how to get into the spirit of the season. He bent down to the tyke's level. "You ready to help me get this tree up?"

Nodding solemnly, Brian held out his toys. "Tools." Then he pointed to his head. "Hat."

"Tell you what," Nash said, adapting the same ultra-serious look as his little helper. "I'll get mine, too."

Nash returned with a real hard hat, small hand saw and tarp. "If everyone will step back, just a bit…"

Callie kept her son safely to the side. Then the two of them watched as Nash pruned. Short minutes later, they had the tree in a stand, a fact that delighted the little boy to no end.

His little chest puffed out proudly, Brian "helped" Nash carry the Christmas tree inside and set it in the living room. Afterward, Callie wrapped a red velour skirt around the base, got out the lights, the star and some unbreakable ornaments in red, green and white. Together, they all worked to decorate the tree. It was the most Christmas Nash'd had in years.

"Pretty." Brian beamed.

"Very Christmassy," Callie decreed.

"It looks great. Thank you." On impulse, Nash enfolded them all in a group hug. "This means a lot to me," he confessed in a low, gruff tone.

To his satisfaction, though she refrained from saying as much, it seemed to mean a lot to Callie, too. Nash relaxed. Maybe this was exactly what the three of them needed. Maybe they were all on their way to having their best Christmas in a very long time.

"HEY THERE, SWEETHEART," Callie's mom said Tuesday morning, when they caught up with each other via phone. "How are things going?"

Callie switched the call to speaker. Aware it was almost time to leave to take Brian to school, she continued loading the breakfast dishes into the dishwasher. "Good." She thought about the last time she'd made love with Nash, and knew it had been so very good.

"Did you have a nice weekend?" Lacey continued.

Callie smiled, reflecting. "Very." Since most of it had been spent with Nash.

"How did your retreat go yesterday?"

"Really well." Callie told her mom the details while she made her son's lunch.

"And the rash on your finger? How is that doing?" Lacey asked with maternal concern.

"It took a few days to fade completely." But after the second time that she and Nash had made love, it had disappeared.

"So no more itching or redness?" her mom prodded.

Callie held out her hand. Her ring finger was smooth as silk. "Nope," she confirmed.

There was the hiss and steam of the coffeemaker in the background. "Have you been able to go back to wearing your rings?"

Callie listened to the distant clatter and knew her mother was filling her thermal work mug and getting ready to leave, too. "They're still at the jeweler's in San Antonio. I haven't had time to pick them up yet."

"Okay. Well, pay attention when you do start wearing them again."

If I start wearing them again, Callie thought.

"Or if the rash comes back before then," her mom warned, sounding more like a physician now than a parent.

Callie and her mom talked a little more. Her mom reiterated how much she was looking forward to seeing them at Christmas.

"Me, too, Mom," Callie said.

Even though it meant leaving Nash behind.

And that, she wasn't so happy about. But, Callie reassured herself, it was only for a couple of days. He'd still be waiting for her when she got back. At least she hoped he would. They hadn't exactly figured out what they had going—except friendship and a blossoming affair.

Time would tell if it turned into anything more. In the meantime, Callie knew, she had to get her son to school.

CALLIE HAD NEVER been one to eavesdrop, but there was something about hearing her name that always stopped her in her tracks. And that morning was no exception.

"Look," Molly Franklin, the head chef of the Double Knot Ranch bakery and catering service said, from inside the party barn, "if Nash Echols were okay with being alone during the holidays, he wouldn't have invited himself to Callie's for Thanksgiving dinner."

Callie's twin, Maggie, spoke up, her voice loud and clear. "It wasn't just him. He asked to bring all the men working for him, too."

"Still," Fiona Sanders said, with maternal wisdom, "it doesn't hurt to welcome Nash back to the community, now that he's here for good."

"And introduce him to all the available women in the area, to boot," Ginny Walker, the new assistant manager, chimed in.

"Well, luckily that doesn't include me," Callie said casually, figuring enough had been said on the subject, and walking in.

"Yes—" her twin sister winked "—since you already know him."

Callie put down her briefcase.

She felt obliged to defend the handsome man they were all conversing about. "I know you-all mean well, but I'm not sure Nash is going to appreciate this."

"Sure he will," Molly Franklin disagreed. "And you

know why? Because single men are always up for a good, hot, home-cooked meal. And that's all everyone who is going to ask him into their domains is going to be offering him."

Fiona Sanders held up her hand. "There's still a lot to be done for the Old-Fashioned Christmas Celebration. So let's get down to business, shall we?"

For the next few hours, Callie concentrated on the tons of details yet to be ironed out.

By the time she left the Double Knot Ranch, it was nearly noon.

She wasn't due to pick Brian up from the Country Day Montessori Preschool until three that afternoon, which gave her plenty of time to stop by her ranch, grab a few things and head for Echols Mountain.

Nash was right where she thought he would be. Halfway up the mountain, in a staked-off area he planned to work in next.

He had sunglasses on to protect against the glare of a partially cloudy winter day. A knit cap covered his shaggy black hair. Black thermal underwear, a pine-green flannel shirt and a khaki field vest covered his massive chest. Worn jeans and brown leather hiking boots cloaked his legs. He had a leather apron stuffed with rolls of scissors, markers, pruning shears and varied colored plastic ribbon slung around his waist. He was unshaven, sexy as all get-out and so very male.

Her heart leaped as she returned his wave and trooped out to join him. It was easy to see what he had been doing. He had been marking trees and other native plants and shrubs for harvest, then recording the results. As she neared, he let the clipboard fall to midthigh. "Hey." He hooked an arm about her shoulder and brought her close enough for a quick, casual kiss to her temple. "Didn't expect to see you today."

She knew it was a little corny, but still… She lifted the wicker basket in her hand. "Thought I would bring you a picnic lunch."

"Thanks, I'm starved."

He put down the gate of his pickup truck and spread a tarp, lifted her up into the bed, removed all his gear— including his hat—and joined her. "You going to stay and eat with me?"

"Why, Nash Echols—" she batted her lashes at him "—I thought you'd never ask."

"So what's up?"

Stalling, Callie handed him an overstuffed turkey, bacon, lettuce and tomato sandwich on sourdough bread. She had hoped to work her way into this.

He watched her pour steaming coffee from a thermos. "You have that look on your face. Like you want to tell me something."

Callie spread a napkin across her lap. "That obvious, hmm?"

"Yup."

While they ate, she relayed the conversation she had overheard. "I saw what they've been doing. They've got a whole social calendar planned for you during the month of December."

Finished with his sandwich, he opened a bag of chips. "Yeah, I know. The invitations have already started coming in."

"So you don't mind?" She found she wasn't nearly as hungry.

Looking more interested in her reaction than what

had gone on behind his back, he leaned against the metal side, legs stretched out in front of him. "That people want to socialize with me? Or that I'm considered a catch in these parts?"

Ah, humor. Was there ever a time when he did not use it to his advantage? "I imagine you're a catch in whatever part of the country you end up in." She tried not to sound as jealous as she actually felt.

His brow lifted. Then his gaze roved her languorously, head-to-toe, before returning to settle on her eyes. "To you, too?"

Callie tried unsuccessfully to fight a blush. "You know I'm attracted to you," she said, doing her best to keep her voice calm and steady. "I think I've made that clear."

He nodded, his expression maddeningly indecipherable. "And I to you."

She sipped her coffee, the heat of the beverage a nice panacea to the lingering chill of the wintry afternoon. "What I can't figure out," she continued, as the sun went all the way behind a cloud, "is why anyone would think you would have trouble finding 'available' women to date all on your own."

Nash drained his cup, crumpled up his napkin and put it in the paper sack she'd provided for trash. "Probably has something to do with Lydia," he said.

An awkward silence fell.

Funny, she hadn't allowed herself to imagine him with another woman. But of course there had been other women.

Was there now, too? Finally, Callie worked up enough courage to ask, "Who is Lydia?"

NASH HAD KNOWN they would have to talk about this sooner or later. Unable to sit still a moment longer, he sighed restlessly and climbed down from the bed of the truck. He paused long enough to give Callie a hand down, too, then walked back out to resume his work. Aware this wasn't an inquiry likely to go away, he said over his shoulder, "Lydia was a woman I dated for five years."

Callie meandered after him, tramping through the undergrowth. "Was she from around here?"

"No." Nash picked up a roll of orange tape and measured off another section of virgin woods. "We met when we were both working in the Pacific Northwest. I brought her home to Texas to propose to her."

Callie ducked beneath the tape to lean up against a particularly sturdy fifty-year-old live oak. "I'm sensing it didn't go well."

"That's putting it mildly."

She shoved her hands in the pockets of her jeans, looking as wary as she had the first time they'd met. He hated seeing her that way.

"And it caught you off guard?" she gathered.

Nash fought the urge to take Callie in his arms and kiss away all her distrust. He also knew it wasn't going to happen unless he gave her the information she was looking for.

Wearily, he shoved a hand through his hair, recounted, "I made it clear from the time Lydia and I first met that I was looking to get married and have a family. She said it was what she wanted, too, once she had established herself in a career."

Callie looked around, found his hat and tossed it to him. "And you believed her."

Inside, Nash's annoyance built. "Yeah, Callie, like a damn fool, I believed her. Right up until the time I got down on my knee, popped the question and she told me that not only did she not want to have kids, but she did not want to actually be married, either."

Callie blinked, for a second looking as confused as he'd felt at the time. "Then why did she ever indicate otherwise?"

Nash sighed. Dropped the roll of tape. Strode nearer. "Because Lydia assumed I was just doing what she had been doing—just saying what people wanted and expected to hear."

Nash paused a moment to let his words sink in.

He looked into Callie's eyes, then matter-of-factly went on, "Lydia was willing to get engaged as long as it never went any further than that. We never got around to actually setting a date or planning a wedding."

Callie rubbed her temples as if she felt a headache coming on. "A lot of people seem to be doing that these days."

He nodded but said nothing.

She trod closer, her eyes soft, serious now. "You must have been really hurt by Lydia's deception."

Nash didn't want her pity. Aware he still felt like a damned fool, he rubbed a hand beneath the stubble on his jaw. He wished he had taken the time to shave that morning. Would have, had he known he would be having lunch with Callie.

He strolled closer. "What made it worse was that I'd told Hart and a few others what I was planning. So when it all went bust, and Lydia went back to Oregon without me, everyone knew what had happened."

Callie wrinkled her nose. "I'm guessing you got a lot of sympathy."

Gazing down at her, he took her hands in his. They were as soft and silky as his were rough and calloused. "Plus well-meaning advice on how to pick 'em next time."

She winced.

Nash let go of her hands. "And that's probably why they all think I need a little 'help' in the romance department." He threaded his fingers through her hair, lifted her face to his. "There is one way to put a halt to all this not-so-subtle matchmaking on my behalf."

"Really?" Color heightened the delicate bone structure of her face. "And what's that?"

Nash took her all the way into his arms. "We could tell everyone I'm already romantically involved. With you."

ANOTHER LONG AWKWARD silence stretched between them.

His pulse accelerating, Nash watched Callie's reaction to his proposal.

Knowing that this was where—if things were really going his way—Callie would leap at the chance to tell everyone they were, if not in love with each other, at least pretty damned smitten.

But if the expression on her face was any indication, he realized with ever-deepening disappointment, she did not want that. Not at all.

Nash pushed aside a sinking feeling of déjà vu. The fact he never seemed able to anticipate when his heart was about to be stomped on. Warning himself not to jump to conclusions, however, he played devil's advocate instead. "Not interested?"

"I'm very interested in you. You know that." Wringing her hands together, she spun around and paced a distance away. Stared down the mountain, to the valley where her ranch sat.

Finally, she turned back to meet his gaze with a level one of her own. "I just like to keep my private life private, that's all. Especially now that I have a son. Plus—" her lower lip quavered "—we haven't…even said…we'd be exclusive. So—"

Nash regarded her in dismay. Was that what was bothering her? She thought what they had was too casual—too inconsequential—to be mentioned?

"You're right." Deciding if it was a fishing expedition she was on, she was going to catch more than she bargained for, he strolled toward her lazily. "We haven't nailed down anything." He caught her around the waist and moved her up against the same broad oak she'd been leaning against earlier.

She caught her breath, and he quantified further, "Yet."

And that, he thought, was mostly because she hadn't seemed to want to do so.

Knowing actions always spoke louder than words, he undid his tool belt and dropped his clipboard. Then, ignoring the look of indignation on her pretty face, he leaned in even closer.

"What are you doing?"

If he didn't know better, he would think it was Callie's heart that was hurting, not her pride. His own body humming with aching, overpowering need, he planted his arms on either side of her so she was pinned between his body and the broad unyielding surface of the oak.

"Making my intentions clear," he told her brazenly, not afraid to put all his cards on the table.

She released an unsteady breath but kept her eyes defiantly on his. "And that is…?"

"To make you my woman." Caught up in something too primal to fight, he kissed her. Once, then again. Until her body softened and she surrendered against him. "I don't care if it's in public or in secret as long as I know that you're the woman for me, and I'm the man for you."

She sighed with pleasure. "I think I could live with that."

It was a start. "Good." He unbuttoned her shirt, unfastened her jeans.

Eyes huge, she whispered, "Here?"

He claimed her supple, hot flesh with the palms of his hands and the pads of his fingertips. "Unless you want to wait?"

His answer came in the speed with which she found his lips, kissed him back. Found the zipper to his jeans.

They kissed again.

And then there was nothing between them but the cold of the outdoors and the heat of their bodies, the swift, searing pleasure that catapulted them to new heights. For once, his control seemed as absent as hers. He didn't hold back, and neither did she. They came, quick and hard. And even after they stopped shuddering, they lingered. Clinging together. Kissing. Prolonging this fierce, intimate experience for as long as possible.

And Nash knew whoever thought Callie was fragile was wrong. She was, in fact, one of the strongest, most resolute women he had ever met.

"Just so you know, I'm going to Frank and Fiona's for dinner this evening," Nash told Callie later, as she was getting ready to leave the woods. "I already said yes. So, if you and Brian want to join me…"

Callie thought about what fun that would be, then the inevitable gossip that would cause, and shook her head. "I meant what I said about keeping this just between the two of us for now. I don't mind everyone knowing we're friends, Nash. That we enjoy hanging out. Or that my son adores you. But beyond that…"

She had a business to run. A past to put all the way behind her. A future to build. She didn't want a hot, sexy love affair detracting from any of that. She didn't want to worry she was jumping headfirst into something else that could leave her emotionally devastated and ripped apart if it ended.

Knowing she would be disappointing him, she cleared her throat and pushed on honestly anyway, "I still want my private life kept private."

He showed no reaction to her decision. "Can I drop by and see you later, then?"

"Sure." Callie nodded, looking down to make sure her buttons were all done up right.

"Although," she added practically, "I can't promise much…" in the way of time or sex "…given how much I have to do."

He walked her to her SUV, lingering long enough to give her a kiss that was so potent, she could barely catch her breath.

"I promise I'll find a way to make myself useful."

"I'm sure you will," she returned dryly. Looping her arms around his neck, Callie kissed him back, knowing she would be counting the minutes until they were together again.

And honestly, if that wasn't proof she was getting in too fast, too deep, yet again, what was?

Chapter Ten

"You look all stressed out," Nash observed the following afternoon when Callie opened the door. Beautiful, but stressed out. When he'd left her the night before—late—after making love again, she had been glowing with happiness. He'd been pretty darned happy, too. But something had obviously changed between then and now.

"What's going on?" he asked in concern.

She let out a beleaguered sigh and reached for his hat and coat. "I took a look at my to-do lists for Christmas a while ago. My work one is reducing nicely, but my personal one is still chock-full of stuff I have yet to tackle."

Nash knew she had scheduled one mother-son activity for every day during the yuletide season. At least it was quiet in the house now—except for the Christmas music playing softly in the background. "What's on the agenda for Brian this evening?"

Callie hooked her arm in his. "He is supposed to be finger painting pictures for both of his grandparents."

Leaning down to kiss her, Nash inhaled a whiff of her perfume. "Let me guess. He's not cooperating?"

Briefly, Callie laid her head on his shoulder. "Actually, the little rascal is overly enthusiastic—*when* I can get him to follow directions——which hasn't been all that often."

She led the way into the playroom adjacent to the kitchen. Brian was standing in front of a child-size easel, a pout of fierce concentration on his face. He was wearing an old adult-size shirt, buttoned up the back. The hem came down past his knees, covering his clothes, and the sleeves were rolled up to just beneath his elbows. A rainbow of colors was splashed all over the paper canvas.

When they walked in, he was focused on the work of art in front of him. The moment he spied Nash, he let out a whoop of pure joy and ran toward him, yelling, "My friend! Here!" at the top of his lungs. Before Callie could intercept him, his hands wrapped around Nash's knees.

Callie gasped as the paint on her son's hands transferred to Nash's pants.

"It's fine," he reassured her good-naturedly, his eyes still on her son. It wasn't often he got such a warm welcome. Was this how dads felt when they came home from work?

Grinning broadly, Nash hefted Brian up into his arms. "How are you, buddy?"

"Good!" Brian transferred even more paint to Nash's shirt and freshly-shaven jaw before smearing more across the collar.

Nash grinned. "Me, too."

Callie groaned at the mess. She rushed to pull a clean cloth from a drawer. "I'm so sorry, Nash."

He wasn't worried about it.

She dampened the cloth beneath the faucet, then came close enough to wipe her resisting son's hands. "The paint is washable. So if you bring your clothes to me tomorrow, I'll launder them for you."

"Nah. I can do it." Reluctantly, Nash set the energetic little boy back on the floor. Brian promptly ran back to his easel. "Look!" He grinned, proud as could be of the abstract art. "For you!"

Callie refolded the damp cloth so only a clean square was visible, then went to intercept her son. "Actually, honey, that's for Grandma Doris and Grandpa Rock."

"No." Brian ripped off the picture before anyone could stop him. "My friend!" He carried it hurriedly to Nash. "Present! You!"

Nash knelt down to receive it in the spirit it was given. "Well, thank you, buddy." He held the still-damp painting to one side and hugged Brian.

"Want to do some more?" Callie asked.

Brian took Nash's hand. "You help."

The next half hour was spent making more paintings. Nash pulled up a chair and worked on one side of the easel while Brian stood on the other. By the time Callie had her son's dinner fixed, Brian had made more paintings for both sets of grandparents. And a third for Nash.

Nash had made some, too.

A colorfully decorated Christmas tree, with presents beneath.

A snowman.

And a ranch house that resembled her own, covered with snow.

And it was only when they were cleaning up that Nash noticed the unexpected addition to the kitchen trash can.

"BRIAN, DID YOU do this?" Callie asked, lifting Seth's photo out of the trash.

Her son walked over, took the plexiglass-framed photo that usually resided next to his bed and promptly pushed it through the swinging top on the kitchen waste can yet again. "All gone," Brian announced, dusting off his hands.

"Honey, that's your daddy's picture." Callie fished it out of the trash yet again.

"No. Away," Brian said, even more emphatically. And that, it seemed, was that.

So while Nash sat with Brian and supervised his dinner, Callie did what she always did when confronted with questions on how to care for her son; she consulted with the resident pediatrician and parenting expert in the family—her mom.

Briefly, she recounted the events to her mother over Skype.

"Was he crying when this happened?" Lacey asked. Home from work, too, she was clad in a casual blouse, jeans and sneakers. She had her bifocals on a chain around her neck. Her short silvery-blond hair was mussed from her long and busy day.

"No. Just frustrated. And determined, as usual."

Her mother's expression gentled. "Maybe you should give any discussions of Brian's daddy a rest for a little bit then. Unless he brings it up specifically."

"Easier said than done when Brian's going around asking every man he sees if he is his daddy. And..."

"What?" On the other end of the connection, her mom continued making a salad for dinner.

Callie swallowed and forced herself to continue, aware she needed advice on this matter, too. "He's starting to get really attached to Nash Echols." *To the point I'm beginning to wish that Nash were Brian's daddy, too. And where would that lead? To more foolish romantic notions? The kind that had pushed her over the edge in the first place?*

"Nash Echols, your nothing-but-trouble next-door neighbor?" her mom asked, her delicate brow furrowed in surprise.

"And friend." And lover. And potential soul mate—if she were ever going to fall in love again.

As loath as she was to lose herself completely in romance ever again, Callie wasn't sure that she even had it in her to fall all the way in love.

Still, there was no denying that Nash was pretty much the exception to every rule she had made for herself upon becoming a widow.

She hadn't needed to make love with him to know that. With effort, Callie forced herself to get back on track. "So, is Brian's behavior cause for concern, Mom?"

"No. Not as long as you respond to what he's telling you and give him the break he needs, while still providing him with a strong and positive male influence in his life..."

Callie breathed a sigh of relief, glad they were still able to talk like this. Video-conferencing made up for being in different parts of the state. "Okay. Thanks, Mom." She smiled her gratitude.

"And, Callie?"

She hesitated, her finger over the disconnect button. "Yes?"

"I know it's an emotional time of year for you. So please proceed with caution when it comes to matters of the heart."

She should have known her mom would see beyond what Callie wanted to reveal; her parents always had been extraordinarily keyed-in to all six of their daughters.

Callie bit her lip, figuring they might as well discuss this, too. "You're afraid I'll get hurt?"

"I'm just saying you're vulnerable, and you have been since Seth died." She hesitated for a long moment, then continued softly, "Therefore, having Brian act out the way he has been just makes you more susceptible."

ALTHOUGH SHE WAS outwardly cheerful, Nash's gut told him that Callie's chat with her mom had upset her on some level. So he asked her about it as soon as Brian had gone to sleep.

Callie settled next to him on the sofa. "She thinks throwing Seth's picture in the trash can is all part of the same phase he's already been going through, and that if I try not to overreact, Brian will relax about not having a daddy, too. At least for the time being."

He draped his arm about her shoulders. Able to feel the residual tension in her body, which hadn't been there when he arrived, hours earlier, he guessed, "You disagree."

Callie turned toward him. "I think the loss is always going to hurt him on some level. I also think it will be easier on Brian if I can figure out a way to give him some sense of his father. Even at this young age. Clearly, a photograph isn't doing it."

Brian savored the warmth of her thigh pressed against his, but tried to keep his libido in check. "Have you tried telling him stories about his dad?"

Frowning, Callie shook her head. "Anything on that level is too abstract for him to grasp. Even if I'm showing him a photo at the same time."

"What about a video?"

She snuggled closer, apparently needing the intimate

physical contact as much as he did. "All I have of him as an adult is our wedding video. And Brian was not the least bit interested in that. He barely made it through the frames of me walking down the aisle on my dad's arm."

Nash chuckled. "That would be a hard sell—for any boy."

"Tell me about it."

He rubbed a silky dark curl between his fingertips. "Would Doris and Rock Grimes have anything?"

Another sigh. "Just film taken when he was much younger. Seth is so young he doesn't look like a daddy to Brian. But—" Callie flashed a wan smile "—I'm sure I'll figure it out eventually."

Nash moved her onto his lap and ran a hand down her spine. "What are you supposed to do in the meantime?"

Callie turned halfway to face him. "Make sure he has positive male influences in his life whom he can interact with. Like Rock, my dad, his uncle Hart…"

He volunteered with a smile. "I'm here, too."

Callie's expression fell. "Which is yet another problem," she admitted, "since Brian clearly ranks you way above every other man in his life thus far."

He studied the turbulent emotion in her blue eyes. "That worries you?"

"What if he gets too attached and then we…" She broke off, unable to finish.

Sensing she was feeling vulnerable again, he wrapped his arms around her. "I'm not going anywhere, Callie."

She bit her lip. "You know what I mean."

He lifted her hand to his lips. "I can see you're scared."

Her expression grew all the sadder. "I let myself view the world far too romantically once, and ended up devastated when everything didn't turn out as optimally as I expected."

"I'm not going to die on you, Callie."

She moved off his lap and wandered over to the Christmas tree. The lights were sparkling every bit as much as the star on top. She paused to adjust a small Snoopy ornament. "You don't know that," she said thickly. Nash rose and crossed to her side. He wrapped his arms around her and tenderly kissed the nape of her neck. "So life is a mystery," he told her, drawing back to look into her eyes. "That doesn't mean we can't have a little faith," he said softly. "And hope. And joy…"

She let out a shuddering breath. "Nash…"

He knew she was fearful of loss. So was he. More than she knew. Forcing himself to find the courage deep within, he kissed her again. "Focus on the present, Callie," he whispered against her mouth. "Focus on this. And how we make each other feel…"

The rest would come.

He was sure of it.

"Well, don't you look gorgeous today," Maggie gushed the following morning when Callie walked into the work party at the Double Knot Ranch. Stations had been set up at some of the banquet tables. Wreath-making at one, assembling yuletide centerpieces at another, gift-wrapping door prizes at a third.

"In fact, you're positively glowing!"

That's what she got for making love all evening long with Nash Echols.

Callie shrugged out of her coat. Comically, she pressed her hand against her cheek and went into a half swoon. "Maybe I'm coming down with a fever."

"Don't joke about that." Fiona Sanders threaded fragrant pine boughs through a metal frame. "The flu epidemic is really starting to take hold in south-central Texas."

"Don't remind me," Maggie moaned. "We've all had our flu shots, except for Hart, who is still putting his off because he's so busy at work."

Fiona scowled. "That son of mine! Do you want me to call him?"

Maggie shook her head. "Hart promised me he would get it sometime in the next week or so."

And Hart always kept his promises, Callie knew.

Just like Nash.

Fiona turned back to Callie. "How are the brochures coming along?"

Callie took a seat at the wreath-making station. She told herself it was because it was a skill she needed to learn, but it was actually because she had come to really love the scent of fresh-cut pine. Maybe because it reminded her of the man in her life.

Forcing her attention back to the business at hand, Callie said, "I've got everyone's done and ready to go to the printers but Nash's."

"What's the hold-up?" Maggie asked.

He's been "distracted," Callie thought silently. *We both have.* "He hasn't given me the old-fashioned photos of the ranch."

"The printer is clamoring for them," Fiona warned.

"I'll get them later today," Callie promised.

"Speaking of Mr. Elusive," Polly said with a lift of her brow. "I hear he's been turning down dinner invitations right and left. Aside from the dinner at your place, Fiona, I don't think he's accepted a single other invitation." She cut off a strand of red Scotch-plaid ribbon and fashioned it into a decorative bow. "You don't think he's depressed, do you?"

Callie kept her head down while she threaded the fresh cut pine boughs through the round metal wreath frame. "Why would he be depressed? He and Lydia broke up several years ago."

Plus, even though he had just taken over the ranch he inherited, his business seemed to be going great.

All eyes turned to Callie. "What do you know about Lydia?" Polly asked.

Me and my big mouth. Callie shrugged as if it were no big deal that he had bared his soul to her. "He mentioned he was almost engaged once."

Another silence fell.

Maggie averted her gaze. A big sign that had Callie wondering if her twin was hiding something, too. She put down her wreath. "What are you-all talking about?"

Abruptly, everyone exchanged glances and clammed up. Like they were afraid to tell her.

Callie waited, not about to let them treat her with kid gloves.

"Because of his family," Fiona said finally.

"The fact they're so far away?" Callie guessed. And promptly realized to her frustration that she had still missed the mark.

"What's going on?" she asked her twin when they were alone. And still got nothing. "What don't I know about Nash?"

Chapter Eleven

Nash opened the door to Callie at four that afternoon, feeling incredibly happy to see her. Unfortunately, it appeared the emotion was not shared.

He inclined his head at the empty space beside her, aware she had a certain cool fire in her eyes that had not been there the day before. Wondering what had happened since they'd seen each other, he moved to let her pass. "I thought you were bringing Brian over."

"I sent him to Maggie's for a playdate instead so we could get right down to business."

Wow. She certainly did not have lovemaking on her mind.

Callie walked into the great room that encompassed half of the first floor. She slipped off her coat and scarf, and draped them over the back of a living room chair. Opened up her briefcase and withdrew a mock-up for a pamphlet, then turned to him with an officious smile. "The promotional brochures we're handing out at the Christmas celebration need to be at the printer tomorrow." She ran her slender fingers over the print. "Here's what I've done for you so far."

He admired the work she had done. "Looks nice."

Callie kept her eyes on the brochure. "Is all the information accurate?"

Curious as to what burr had gotten under her saddle, he read through the history of the Echols Mountain Ranch Christmas tree operation as well as a brief summary of his plans for the future.

It was as perfect as he had expected, and he told her so, adding, "I like what you've done with the color photos I provided of the mountainside. And the close-up of an actual tree, grown here." He tapped the blank space. "But what's supposed to go here?"

"Two photos from back in the day."

Nash swore inwardly. He'd been so caught up in his budding relationship with Callie, he'd forgotten all about that.

Callie squared her slender shoulders. "I know we talked about you getting a couple for me."

The last thing he wanted to do, when the present was going so well, was go digging through his family's past.

"Do we really need them?"

"If we're to keep with the 1880s theme and the look of every other brochure we're producing for the celebratory event, yes, we do. Unless…" Callie paused, her expression suddenly cagey. "There's some reason you don't want to touch on the past?" Nash sighed. So her brusque attitude was founded in something else. "Who have you been talking to?"

A glimmer of hurt flashed in her eyes. "That's just it." Callie exhaled slowly. "No one will tell me anything. At least not outright. But it's clear something happened here that has everyone worried about you during the holiday season." She held up a hand before he could interrupt. "And it's not anything to do with your breakup with Lydia, either. So don't pretend that it is."

"I'd really rather not go there," Nash said, setting the pamphlet aside. *Not during the holiday season.* He caught her around the waist and pulled her close.

Callie splayed her hands across his chest. "So you'd prefer to keep things purely superficial between us?"

Emotion rose. "There's nothing superficial about the way I view you or our relationship," he told her softly, threading a hand through her hair.

Disbelief tightened the corners of her mouth. She extricated herself, her resentment clear. "If that's true, then prove it. Here and Now. Tell me the truth."

CALLIE'D HAD ONE relationship that was built on fantasy, whimsy and her and Seth's mutual vision of romantic perfection. And while it had been fun while it lasted, such careful idealism hadn't served her well when she was left on her own to pick up the pieces.

If there was tragedy or hurt in Nash's past, powerful enough to make him shut down emotionally, she had to know about it. Otherwise, things would never work out between them.

He gave her a look that told her a wall was already going up around his heart. "We all have our sad stories to tell, Callie. It doesn't mean we have to ruin Christmas by dwelling on the past pain."

There was a time in her life when she had believed that if something wasn't wonderful, it didn't warrant her time or attention. Living that way, however, had left her woefully unprepared to deal with the harder facets of life.

"So in other words," she said, so disappointed she

could barely look him in the eye, "you're shutting me out, too?"

"We can talk about it later."

She knew an evasion when she saw one. "When? January?"

He shrugged, but said nothing more. Clearly, at least in his view, they were done with this conversation.

Outside, the wind picked up. In the few minutes she had been inside his home, the sky had grown dark and gray.

Aware she could not—would not—live this way again, Callie shut her briefcase. Then picked up her coat. "Like I said…I need those photos, Nash." She ignored him as he moved to help her with her wrap. "So if you want to get them for me now."

He did not move.

Which figured. When Nash did not want to do something, he was as unmovable as a two-ton boulder.

Fighting the insane urge to pull him into her arms and hold him close, until everything real—and potentially upsetting—went away, Callie swallowed. "Or if you could scan them into your computer and email them to me by tomorrow morning, at the latest, I'd appreciate it."

Something flickered in his eyes. Disappearing before she could even begin to identify it.

Aware there was nothing more to be said, Callie looped her scarf around her neck and walked out the door. She left, still upset Nash had refused to confide in her. Not sure where to go from there.

And she was still wondering whether she should try to get closer to him or take a big step back when he appeared at her doorstep at nine-thirty that evening. His hair was mussed, as if he'd been running his hands through it. His lips set, strong jaw stubbled with shadow. But it was his turbulent dark silver eyes and stark expression that sent an arrow into her heart.

"Brian asleep?" he asked.

The need to comfort him as fierce as her yearning to see him, Callie nodded. She ushered him in, aware he looked like he'd been through hell in the hours that had ensued. "For hours now."

He handed her a manila envelope. "You'll find everything you want to see inside."

She opened it while he hung his coat, walked over and stoked up the fire in the grate.

There were fading color photographs of a fifty-year-old man standing in front of the Echols Mountain ranch house he currently occupied—albeit a much smaller version of the same log-cabin-style dwelling. "Is this your great-uncle?"

Nash nodded fondly. "Ralph Echols."

The next photo was of Nash, at the beginning of his teen years. Beside him was a kid several inches shorter, with the same thick black hair, rugged broad-shouldered physique and handsome facial features. "Is this your cousin?"

"My younger brother, Rob. He died a few months after that was taken. He was twelve. I was fourteen."

"Oh, Nash." In that moment, he looked so battle-weary, she wanted to cry.

He shoved his hands in his pockets, his body posture indicating he wanted to keep a physical distance between them. "We always went to Colorado over the Christmas holidays," he recounted in a flat, expressionless voice. "My brother and I would head for the slopes while our parents relaxed by the fire."

His jaw tightened. Regret came into his eyes.

Nash swallowed and pushed on. "Because I was older I was supposed to watch out for my kid brother, but Rob was so reckless, and it was impossible to get him to listen to me."

Callie listened with mounting unease.

Nash shook his head, began to pace. "Anyway, we had just gotten snowboards, and we weren't very good with them yet, but Rob insisted we tackle one of the tougher trails anyway."

He paused, mouth flattening, shoulders hunching, as if to protect against the pain. "I should have just said no, but I knew if I did, Rob'd probably just take off and go it alone. So I went with him."

As a good brother should.

Another silence fell.

Nash's gaze grew distant. "A quarter way down the mountain, Rob spun out of control. Went head over heels and landed hard on the edge of his board. His windpipe was crushed and he died instantly."

Oh, my God. "Nash."

"My parents never got over it. And of course they blamed me for not being able to prevent it."

"It wasn't your fault.

"Anyway, after that, my folks never wanted to celebrate Christmas again. So for the rest of the time I was in high school, we always went somewhere else—like the Caribbean—and pretended it didn't exist." He exhaled, regret mixing with sorrow and hurt. "I figured my mom and dad would get over it, come to realize that they still had one son left, but their mourning only got worse as time went on."

He turned to her, the hurt in his eyes so fathomless she felt her own heart turn inside out.

He came toward her. "I couldn't live in a perpetual state of grief. And I sure didn't want to be in the shadow of my brother's ghost for the rest of my days. So they moved to Japan and I stayed here and we talk once, maybe twice, a year. And that's it."

Callie took his hand in hers. "And your great-uncle?"

Nash took her other hand, too. "Was family to me— the only family I had left. And now he's gone, too." He let his gaze fall briefly to their intimately entwined fingers before meeting her eyes again. "Which is why I guess the locals are so worried about me. Because they all know what happened."

Callie wrapped her arms around his waist. Still holding him close, she tilted her head back and searched his face. "But you don't think they need to be?"

He drew her closer without hesitation. "I'm not going to tell you my brother's death doesn't still hurt," he told her quietly. "It does. And it probably always will."

He threaded one hand through her hair. The other remained clasped tightly around her waist.

Acceptance radiated in his expression. "But I'm not going to let that one tragedy dominate the rest of my life. And I'm sure as hell not going to let it ruin every holiday I have from here on out."

He paused to look deep into her eyes. "Christmas is an affirmation of everything positive in this life. I intend to celebrate it every year with every fiber of my being."

The warmth of his body seeped into hers.

"Which is why I don't like to talk about or dwell on what happened in the past. But," he added, with raw apology, "me not telling you created a wedge between us."

He shook his head. "I don't want that, either," he said gruffly. "Not when things are starting to go so well."

"I don't, either." Callie moved closer. She caught his face in her hands and their lips fused together in a fiercely emotional kiss. "Nash…" Tears blurred her eyes for all he had been through.

"Let's live in the moment, Callie. Let's celebrate the joy of the season and have faith that everything will work out."

She knew he had not come here to make love to her this evening, and that made the culmination of everything they needed, everything they felt, all the sweeter.

And when at last they came back to earth, she felt closer to Nash than ever. And for now, she realized contentedly, that was gift enough.

"ARE YOU SURE you want to do all this?" Nash asked several days later. He strolled into her kitchen, looking tall and indomitable.

Aware that once again, all his raw male power was focused on her, wreaking havoc with her senses, Callie rushed around, trying to simultaneously pack a picnic supper and get their Christmas cards ready to mail.

She handed Nash a stack of envelopes to finish sealing. "I am very sure."

"Because?"

Aware his laissez-faire attitude and rakishly sexy presence could easily sidetrack her into doing something naughty, she worked on trying to find enough postage stamps to keep him busy and her mind where it should be—on the upcoming holiday.

"I've been so busy this week, I've gotten way behind on my list of the Christmas events and activities that I want Brian to experience," she explained. "So this is the only way I can think of to work it all in."

Nash stood at the counter next to her, casually sealing and stamping.

"Besides—" she brought out the wicker hamper, too "—Brian doesn't have school today. My in-laws are coming tomorrow, and they have offered to babysit while they're in town so I can get my own shopping or whatever I need to do done."

Finished, he lounged next to her, arms folded in front of him. Even in a sweater and jeans, he looked impossibly sexy.

"That look tells me you have something specific in mind."

Aware they had managed to make love every day they had been together, Callie basked in the warm familiarity of his gaze. Which was, she admitted, yet another reason why she was so behind this year. She wrinkled her nose at him. "Let's just say 'the elves' may need some assistance putting things together."

His eyes drifted over her. "Looking for volunteers?"

Callie grinned. "Always."

Nash caught her hand and reeled her in. Despite herself, she found herself melting against him when he bent down and kissed her tenderly.

Small shoes clattered in the hall. Nash lifted his head and let Callie go just before Brian came dashing in.

"My friend!"

Nash responded by scooping Brian up into his arms. "What do you know," he teased, "it's *my* friend, Brian!"

Brian beamed, looped his arms around Nash's neck and gave him a big hug. "Go. With?" he asked.

Callie grabbed her son's jacket and knit cap. "Yes.

Nash is going with us to see the Christmas All Over the World exhibit at the children's museum. After that we're going to have a picnic dinner in the park, and hear the outdoor concert put on by the all-city children's choir. And then on the way home we'll take the drive-through Christmas lights display at Santa's Ranch."

"Santa Claus," Brian repeated, smiling.

"Which reminds me," Callie said, "we still have to write a letter to him, too."

As it turned out, though, to her disappointment, not everything went according to plan.

The museum was so crowded Brian had a hard time seeing anything, even when Nash lifted him up in his arms.

He wanted his dinner way before the outdoor concert was due to start, and then was so excited and restless he barely ate a thing.

He shouted so loudly during the performance they had to leave. And fell asleep long before they ever reached the last destination.

Nash caught a glimpse of her slumbering child in the rearview mirror as they fell into line behind a huge string of cars waiting to get into Santa's Ranch. "What do you want to do?" he asked.

Callie sighed, aware she had never been so exhausted. Or frustrated. "Head home, if that's okay with you."

"Sounds good."

Unfortunately, Brian woke up when they were getting him out of the car. Cranky and overtired, he burst into tears that Callie could not soothe. A feeling of failure overwhelming her, tears flooded her eyes, too. Nash caught her glance, then held out his arms to her son, creating enough of a diversion for Callie to pull herself together. A sobbing Brian went into Nash's embrace, and together they went into his room and got him ready for bed.

Although Callie had regained her usual composure by then, Brian still wanted Nash to rock him. So he sat down in the glider and cuddled the little boy close. Sighing contentedly, Brian wreathed his arms around Nash's shoulders and rested his head in the crook of Nash's neck.

Tearing up all over again at the unbearably tender sight, Callie slipped from the room.

Eventually, Nash joined her.

He was so calm and reassuring. It was no wonder her son adored him and wanted Nash for a daddy.

In Brian's place, Callie would have wanted Nash, too.

Aware the void in her little boy's life was only going to get bigger as years passed, Callie asked, "He asleep?"

Nash nodded. Understanding only part of the reason behind her dejected mood, he sank down on the sofa beside her and sent her a sympathetic glance. "Parenting is hard work."

Callie absorbed the heat of his body pressed up against hers. *You got that right.* "Some days, like today, are harder than others. And for the record," she forced herself to voice the mea culpa, "you were right in your estimation of my plans. It was too much."

Nash draped his arm around her shoulders. Pressed a kiss in her hair. "He's two and a half, Callie. I think he had a good time."

"I just don't want him to feel shortchanged because it's Christmas and he doesn't have a dad."

He gave her a reassuring squeeze. "You do more than most two parents combined that I've ever seen." He paused. "Want some advice?"

Callie winced. "I have a feeling you're going to give it to me whether I want it or not."

He slid a finger beneath her chin and turned her to face him. "Ease up a little. Let Brian enjoy the small things."

She smiled wistfully. There was so much comfort to be gained just from being here with Nash, like this. It made her long to be married again. "Like cookie baking and decorating?"

"Or just cookie eating."

Callie rolled her eyes. She let her head drop to the back of the sofa then threw her forearm across her brow. "You're such a man."

He chuckled at her comical "Oscar-worthy" performance. "You're such a mom."

She straightened. Turned serious. "For the record, Nash Echols. I'm glad you're here."

"Want to know something?" he returned softly, kissing her yet again. "So am I. This is the best holiday season I've had in a very long time."

Chapter Twelve

"We still on for tonight?" Nash asked the next morning when he stopped by to have breakfast with the two of them. Being here was a great way to start off his day. Especially when Callie looked so darned beautiful and welcoming.

He could tell that, like him, she wasn't long out of the shower. Her dark curls were still slightly damp, and smelled of the flowery shampoo she used. Her ivory skin was smooth and flawless, her cheeks tinged with pink. But it was the lively light in her deep blue eyes—the one that indicated she was considering kissing him again—that really drew him in.

His spirits soaring, Nash lounged against the counter, watching as Callie stood at the stove and poured pancake batter onto the griddle.

She met his glance and nodded in answer to his question. "Yes. My in-laws will be here at three. I want to spend a little time with them, too, but should be free to leave here around six this evening."

Sounded good to Nash. "How about I come pick you up then?" he asked, as Brian ran over to him and held out his arms, indicating he wanted to be picked up.

Callie smiled as Nash hoisted her son in his arms.

"Wouldn't it be easier for me to drive to your ranch, since all the things that need assembling—" she continued talking in a code only the "grownups" could comprehend "—are going over there this morning?"

"Whatever you think is best." Noting that Callie had her son's breakfast ready, Nash carried him over to the booster seat and set him down. When Brian was centered in the cushioned insert, he slid the big chair closer to the table. "Do you have a curfew this evening?"

"Um, no." Callie poured a little syrup on her son's plate and handed him a fork. "Not really." With Brian eating, she returned to the stove. She looked at Nash, speaking in code once again. "Doris and Rock already know it's going to take however long it takes to do that stuff."

And anything *else* we might get around to, Nash thought mischievously.

Callie continued, "They're going to go on to bed at their usual time, which is around ten."

Nash accepted the mug she handed him and poured himself a cup of coffee. "Well, then, since you have an actual babysitter, how about you and I make it a date?"

Which was something, up to this point, they hadn't actually had.

Callie paused then squinted at him uncertainly. "To put together stuff?"

"To have a grown-up dinner first, just the two of us— in San Antonio. And then put together stuff. Or I can do the assembling this afternoon at my place. Then you and I can just have the grown-up dinner on the River Walk." Which was, he admitted, what he really wanted. Uninterrupted time alone with Callie.

She handed him a plate with a piping hot stack of buttermilk pancakes. "You really wouldn't mind all that direction reading and so on?"

He shrugged. "I love that stuff." Sitting down at the kitchen table, he spread some whipped butter over the stack, drizzled some maple syrup on top and then dug in. "Seriously, anything I can do to make your holiday a joyous one is great with me."

"Well…" Callie regarded him happily. "I really do suck at that kind of stuff. I'm always putting things on upside down and backward."

He chuckled, glad he had won her over. "Then it's a date?"

"Yes." Callie brought her own plate to the table and sat opposite him. She wrinkled her nose. "As long as we don't refer to it as that to anyone else."

Somehow, Nash wasn't surprised she remained cautious. Lifting a shoulder, he watched her over the rim of his coffee mug. "So it will be a secret date."

His teasing brought a flush to her cheeks. "Do you mind keeping our private life private?" She searched his eyes.

"Not at all."

It was enough she had officially agreed to go out with him.

Because that was one step closer to where he wanted to be. Nash grinned. Who said Christmas didn't come early?

NASH COMPLETED THE tasks for Callie, as promised, then dressed as they had agreed he would. Happy to be spending the evening with her, he headed for the ranch next door.

"Well, hello, Nash!" Doris Grimes opened the door. "Come on in. Callie's running a little late this evening."

Rock Grimes came forward to shake Nash's hand, too. "Good to see you, son. You're quite the hero around here."

Hero? Nash kept his expression inscrutable. He strolled into the living room. "Callie said that?"

"Didn't have to." Rock beamed. "We could see it in her eyes. And of course little Brian can't stop talking about you, either. It's 'my friend Nash this,' and 'my friend Nash that.'"

That wasn't such a big surprise. Nash couldn't stop talking about Brian, either. He was such a cute kid. As for Callie, well, was there a moment in the day when she wasn't on his mind…?

Aware Callie's in-laws were waiting for his reaction, Nash returned pleasantly, "It's nice to have such great neighbors. And nice to see the two of you again."

Weary of the grown-up conversation, Brian ran up to his grandfather. "Are you my daddy?" he asked Rock.

Giving Rock no chance to reply, Brian hammed it up and shook his head dramatically, as if enacting a scene from his favorite storybook. "No. *You're* not my daddy."

Brian ran up to Doris and comically repeated the same thing.

The coatrack was next. Then the grandfather clock. Finally, Brian turned to Nash and, arms spread wide, said with complete and utter confidence, "*You're* my daddy!"

Silence fell.

Talk about an uncomfortable moment, Nash thought, given the fact that Rock and Doris were Seth's parents. To their credit, though, they seemed to accept their grandson's clowning around as the mischievousness that it was meant to be.

Figuring the best way to put an end to it was to react in kind, Nash scooped Brian up into his arms. "No," he declared, pointing his finger at the center of the little boy's chest. "*You* are *my* daddy!"

Brian burst into gales of laughter that soon had everyone chuckling, too. "No!" he proclaimed, flushing and shaking his head. "I not your daddy! I little boy."

"Yes, you are, and a cute little dickens at that." Nash gave Brian another hug, silently beseeching him to let the search for an acceptable daddy go—at least for the evening—then attempted to transfer him to his grandfather.

Brian reacted by holding on to Nash a little tighter.

Again, neither of Seth's parents seemed to mind. "Why don't you come in and sit down," Doris invited. "We can get to know each other better while you're waiting for Callie to come downstairs."

Nash sat on the sofa. "Sure." Although it suddenly felt as awkward as his teen years when he had arrived to pick up a date.

"I gather you're not married," Rock said.

Brian slid onto the floor, picked up two toy construction trucks and brought them back to the sofa. He kept one and gave the other to Nash.

"No, I'm not married," he replied genially, resurrecting his best poker face. What had Callie told them about their plans for the evening anyway?

"Would you like to be?" Doris asked.

Bored, Brian settled on Nash's lap and worked at undoing the knot of his tie. "Married? Yes, I would," Nash said. *Especially if the bride in question were Callie.*

"What about kids?" Rock persisted. "Any plans there?"

Another easy question. "I love them. I'd like to have some."

"Any particular number?" Doris smiled.

"Definitely more than one," Nash said.

Brian yawned and snuggled close to Nash. He cuddled the little boy close in return.

Abruptly, Callie appeared in the door.

She was dressed in a cranberry-red suit and heels, her cloud of dark-chocolate curls beautifully encircling her face. She had a briefcase in hand. "Ready?" she asked in a brisk, professional tone.

Nash kissed the top of Brian's head before setting him down. Stood.

"I go?" Brian asked plaintively, clinging to Nash's leg.

"No, honey, this is a business meeting." Callie picked up her son and danced him around the room. "But you are going to have fun with Grandma Doris and Grandpa Rock tonight. I promise…"

A smiling Doris and Rock distracted Brian so Nash and Callie could take their leave. When they were completely out of earshot, he echoed, *"Business meeting?"* He had assumed she would say they were going out either as friends or to meet friends. Not this.

He held the door for her, aware all over again just how beautiful she was.

"Trust me," she said, her manner as formal as her words. Looking past his shoulder, she waved at the threesome standing in the window, then climbed gracefully into the cab of his pickup truck. "This is for the best."

"This is actually a great time for me to go over the suggestions I have compiled to help advertise the expansion of your business," Callie told Nash once they were en route to the city.

While he drove, she talked. By the time they reached downtown San Antonio, she had talked about each option in depth. "Of course, I've written it all down for you," she said. "So you'll be able to take it home later and review it at your leisure."

"Great job," he said.

"So what was the interrogation from my in-laws about?" she asked, once they were strolling along the River Walk. It had been beautifully decorated for the holidays. Thousands of twinkling lights formed a glittering canopy overhead. Long rows of glowing luminaries lined the walkways. On the river that cut through the heart of the city, boatloads of carolers and bands serenaded them.

Looking resplendent in a dark suit, striped shirt and tie, Nash took her hand in his. He had shaved closely. Maybe gotten a haircut, too. "I think they were trying to figure out how marriageable a guy I am."

Callie moved in closer, to avoid a group coming their way on the sidewalk. Nash responded by curving an arm about her waist and pressing a kiss to the top of her head.

"And the result was…?" Callie asked, trying not to get too caught up in the brisk masculine scent of him.

Aware they were still a little early for their dinner reservation, he took her up to one of the stone arches that overlooked the river below. He lounged against the side of the walking bridge and looked down at her. "They seemed to approve. They sure didn't appear to mind when Brian was facetiously claiming me as his daddy. I have to tell you…" He paused, shook his head. "I wasn't sure how that was going to go over. Their late son actually being Brian's father, and all."

Callie had been nervous about it, too—unnecessarily it had turned out. "They know how hard I've worked to give Brian some sense of his dad. They also know I may have come up with a solution."

He lifted a brow, listening intently.

Callie drew a breath and pushed on. "I'm going to make a video like the ones they show about the bride and groom at rehearsal dinners, and have it set to music. It will only run a couple of minutes, but I think it will be more engaging to Brian than a simple photo."

He kept his eyes locked with hers. "That's a good idea."

Bolstered by his support, she continued, "Doris, Rock and I were working on it this afternoon, going through some old photos. And I think I have the ones I'm going to use."

"That should help."

"I hope so." Callie sighed, then pushed on to the more difficult part of the conversation. Once again, she lifted her gaze to his, and kept it there. "In the meantime, Doris and Rock really want me to get married again."

A wealth of feeling was in his eyes. "To anyone in particular?"

"Yes. You."

He stared at her a long silent moment. Then leaned closer once again, inundating her with the tantalizing, masculine scent of his cologne. "You're kidding."

Suddenly, she was having trouble catching her breath. "I wish I was."

His voice dropped a seductive notch. "They barely know me."

She gazed into his eyes, adding even more softly,

"They feel they know enough about the important things."

Incredulity mixed with the concern on his face.

"You have a good reputation within the community and the business world," Callie continued, figuring for all their sakes she should tell him everything she had learned. "Yes, they are pragmatic enough to have had you checked out by their attorney."

"Wow."

She had never seen so many expressions cross his face in one minute. Shock. Disbelief. Wariness. Joy. "They're impressed by how attached Brian is to you already."

"I care about him, too, you know that," he interjected gruffly, squeezing her hand.

"And—" she drew a quavering breath, ignoring the warmth spiraling through her "—they can see there is a basic attraction between you and me. Enough of one to build a relationship on, in their view."

He closed the distance between them and gazed at her as if she were the sexiest, most desirable woman on earth. "What about love?"

Callie's heart thundered in her chest. "They don't expect me to duplicate what I had with Seth with anyone else. But they do think both Brian and I would be a lot happier if we had a man in our lives, and to them, at least, you are the perfect candidate."

His eyes crinkled at the corners and his lips took on a mischievous tilt. "How so?"

Callie shrugged, aware they were headed into dangerous territory here.

"You already live next door." She did her best to maintain her pragmatic attitude. Not easy, when all she could think about at the moment was kissing him again.

"You're committed to the land and the business you inherited, just as I am committed to my new venture." She paused to wet her suddenly dry lips and saw his eyes track the movement in return.

"Brian loves you. And you adore him in return. And like I said, they have noticed there is a physical chemistry, as well as a budding friendship." And like her, had difficulty figuring out a reason why she shouldn't get closer to this big strapping man. Maybe even come to depend on him…in the same way she had once depended on their son.

Nash put his hands on her shoulders and gently ran them down the length of her arms, to her hands. He peered down at her. "What do your parents think of all this?"

"The exact opposite. They urged me to be cautious and not leap into anything, given the enormity of my loss and the fact that I'm still in a 'vulnerable' state."

He searched her face, then asked huskily, "What do you think?"

I don't want to make the same mistakes I made when I was married to Seth and overly romanticize things to the point I lose sight of myself and my ability to stand on my own.

But, not wanting to get into a discussion about her late husband, she simply said, "I don't want to think. I just want to spend time with you."

And make love with you. And not worry about the future and all the things that could go wrong if I tie myself to you the way I tied myself to Seth.

All of a sudden, the grin was back on his handsome face. He lifted her hands to his lips and kissed the back of her knuckles, in turn. "Sounds good to me."

On impulse, she wound her arms around his neck, went up on tiptoe and kissed him tenderly. "Then how about this?" she proposed softly. Nearby a mariachi band broke into the cheerful melody of "Feliz Navidad." "Why don't you and I be each other's Christmas present—to each other?"

Nash kissed her back gently, lovingly. "You've got yourself a deal…"

"Santa's workshop is coming along nicely," Maggie observed from the corner of the Double Knot party barn on Thursday afternoon, where the setup for the Christmas celebration was taking shape.

Callie grinned, admiring the sight of Nash in rugged work clothes and a tool belt jangling around his waist as he helped fasten the various parts of the North Pole into shape.

"Good thing we have so many big strapping Texas men to help."

"Speaking of the one in your life, how are things with Nash?" Maggie asked.

Callie went back to draping cranberry-red tablecloths over the tables. He had become so much a part of her life in the past four weeks, it was astounding. "Fine."

Maggie added the centerpieces—tall hurricane glasses with thick white candles, surrounded by pretty red-and-green wreaths. "I mean, really."

No use pretending; her twin knew her thoughts and feelings almost before she did. "So good it scares me," Callie admitted quietly.

With her last event for the month over, and his schedule relatively freed up, the two of them had had plenty of time to spend together. To the point they found a reason to be together at least once every day.

"I hear you're helping him devise ways to market the extension of his business into xeriscape plants and lumber."

After the tablecloth was situated, Callie replaced the chairs. "Yes. I think he's going to be enormously successful."

Maggie moved on to the next table along with Callie. "So, why haven't you told everyone you're dating?"

Callie focused on her task, rather than her twin's assessing look. "Because we're not dating exactly," she protested. "We're just hanging out a lot as friends." *And lovers.*

Maggie regarded her with sisterly affection. "Well, just don't wait too long to let him know how you really feel. Otherwise, he's likely to think you aren't as serious about him as *I know* you are."

To Callie's relief, the rest of the day passed quickly. It pleased her to no end that preparations for the celebration were coming together so well.

Finally, right before they all headed home, costumes for everyone working the event were passed out. Maggie's husband, Hart, got two.

The first, the same "Texas gambler" all the men were wearing. The second, a complete Santa ensemble.

"Now be sure you keep this under wraps," Fiona Sanders told her son. "We don't want Henry to guess his daddy is going to be Old St. Nick when the time comes."

Hart grinned. "Mum's the word, Mom."

Callie turned to Nash. Garment bags looped over their arms, they walked out to their vehicles, which were parked side by side. "You don't think Brian will recognize his uncle, do you?"

Nash held her costume for her while she unlocked her SUV. "If anyone can pull it off, Hart can." He leaned past her to put it in the cargo area.

Callie followed him over to his truck. She watched as he opened up the rear passenger door. "That's not really an answer."

Nash leaned across the seat to lay his bag flat. "You want me to be blunt?"

She tore her eyes from his firmly muscled thigh. "I'm not sure…"

He removed his tool belt, set it on the floor in front of the seat and then straightened to his full six foot two inches. "Your son is one of the brightest little kids ever put on this earth. Under normal circumstances, not much gets by him."

True, Callie knew.

Nash flashed an inviting grin. "On the other hand, he can be as starstruck as everyone else. And once he gets a load of all that fake snow, the glittering trees, the elves from the high school drama department and the big guy in the white beard and glasses and red suit, it will probably be all he can do to tell Santa what he wants for Christmas."

Callie relaxed at the reassuring words. "You're right. That will be okay. What might not be is Brian's preschool party tomorrow."

Accurately sensing she had something important to say, Nash waited.

Drawing a deep breath, Callie pushed on, "Most of the other kids are going to have a mom and a dad there for them. Unfortunately, neither of Brian's grandfathers are available. Hart will be there—for Henry—and could sort of step in for Brian as his uncle, at least part of the time, but..."

"You're worried Brian is going to pick up on the fact that he doesn't have a daddy again. And be upset about it."

Callie nodded. Tears pressed at the back of her eyes. "This is the first Christmas he's ever had where he's really aware of what's going on. I really want it to be a good one for him." Nash's expression gentled. Because there were others around them, heading to their vehicles, he didn't touch her, but he might as well have. She felt his tender concern that intensely. "You want me to go—as his friend?"

And mine, Callie thought.

But aware they were still in a place where they could be overheard, Callie only smiled and responded as casually as possible, "I know it would mean the world to him—" and to me "—if you could."

Chapter Thirteen

"What's wrong with Hart?" Callie asked her sister during the preschool party Friday afternoon.

Maggie refilled the punch bowl. "He's had a throbbing headache all day."

Callie set out a platter of vanilla cupcakes, decorated with green and red frosting holly berries. "He's not getting the flu, is he?" It had been going around.

"He thinks it's just dehydration and lack of sleep. He worked at the Double Knot all day yesterday, then headed up security for a rock star doing a concert in San Antonio last night."

"What time did he get home?"

"Four o'clock in the morning."

"Ouch."

"Yeah. He wasn't supposed to work last night but one of his employees had a sick child, so Hart took his place."

Callie recalled, "And he hasn't had his shot, has he?"

"Actually, he did get it. The problem is it takes two weeks to be fully effective, and he was just vaccinated a couple of days ago."

"Well, hopefully, lack of sleep is all it is."

"From your lips…" Maggie grinned, watching her husband help Henry polish off the last of their pizza.

Nash did the same for Brian. Finished, the four joined the Clean Plate Club and headed over to the table to claim their dessert.

Unable to resist, Callie called out as they passed, "Having fun?"

Nash nodded.

Brian patted Nash's hand. "My friend here, Mommy."

"I can see that, honey," Callie said with a satisfied smile.

When Brian's teacher headed their way, the little boy grabbed Nash's hand. "Go me." Proudly, Brian led Nash over to converse with Mrs. O'Reilly.

And so it went. Brian took Nash to meet all his friends and their dads.

And Callie knew she had been right to invite Nash to be here for Brian. It seemed to mean a lot to both of them. It was certainly doing a lot to fill her with the Christmas spirit...

Beside her, Maggie asked, "What's Nash doing for the holiday?"

"I'm not sure," Callie murmured. She'd been wondering the same thing herself. "He mentioned he has a lot of invitations—he always does this time of year."

"If I were you..." Maggie suggested meaningfully.

Callie lifted her palm. "I know what you'd do," she told her twin.

However, that didn't mean *she* was ready to put *her* heart on the line that way. It was way too risky. Still, she did enjoy spending time with Nash. So very much...

By the time they left the school, dark blue clouds were visible on the horizon.

Callie studied the sky with a sigh. "There's the Blue Norther coming in." A chill was already in the air. She turned to Nash. "I hope it doesn't rain tomorrow. A winter storm would ruin a lot of what we have planned for the Old-Fashioned Christmas Celebration. Especially the train rides up Sanders Mountain to Nature's Cathedral, where the caroling and sing-alongs are supposed to take place."

Nash helped Brian get situated in his car seat, then held the driver door open for Callie. "The party starts at ten and concludes at 4:00 p.m.—an hour and a half before dark. Precipitation isn't expected until six tomorrow evening, at the earliest. And with the temperature still in the midthirties, all it's going to be is rain."

Impressed, Callie climbed behind the wheel of her SUV. "You've been checking the weather report, too?"

"Hey," he teased, settling into the passenger seat beside her, his big body filling the compartment with laudable ease. "We have to have Mother Nature on our side." He angled a thumb at the center of his broad chest and regarded her with a devilish glint in his eye. "And I think she will be, it being Christmas and all."

Callie smiled, aware how much like "family" they already felt at this moment. What would it be like, she wondered wistfully, if they ever became one? For real?

"See Santa?" Brian piped up from his car seat, interrupting her thoughts.

"Yes." When they reached a stop sign, Callie turned briefly to look at her son. "Santa—" or in other words, Uncle Hart "—is coming to the party tomorrow."

"Sit lap," Brian said.

Callie nodded and resumed her driving. "Yes, you and all the other children are going to have a chance to sit on Santa's lap and tell him what you want him to bring you for Christmas."

Nash shifted as much as his seat belt would allow and looked at her son. "What are you going to ask Santa for, buddy?" he asked curiously.

Tensing, Callie braced herself for him to say, "A daddy."

Instead, her son offered a toothy grin. "Tractor!" he said. "Sit on."

"WHAT ARE WE going to do?" Callie said several hours later, after they had finished dinner and put her exhausted son to bed. Still in the black wool skirt, tights and red cashmere sweater she had worn to the preschool party, she ambled into the living room with Hart at her side. "I had no idea Brian wanted a play tractor to ride on. I thought all he wanted was the play-construction stuff."

Nash had shed his sport coat and tie when they got to her place. While helping her with dinner, dishes and the bedtime routine, he'd undone the first two buttons of the pale blue oxford shirt and rolled up the sleeves to just below the elbows. With the hint of evening shadow lining his jaw, he looked rumpled and sexy in the way of all devoted dads. Except he wasn't Brian's daddy. Or even a permanent fixture in her life. She just wished he was.

Oblivious to the increasingly possessive nature of her thoughts, Nash pulled up a chair and sat down at her desktop computer in the living room. "It's still six days to Christmas. We've got plenty of time to make sure all of Brian's wishes come true." Ready to make that happen, he hit the on button on Callie's desktop.

Her computer had been in sleep mode. The screen lit up with what she had last been working on.

The montage of Seth through the years. There were

forty pictures, thumbnail size. Some of them featured Seth as an adult, but most of them were of Seth and Callie.

Callie had to hand it to Nash. She drew in a quick rueful breath, because it felt as if she had just seen a ghost, but he didn't so much as blink.

"Sorry," he said, voice neutral as his low-key expression. Avoiding her eyes, he started to rise. "I should have asked first."

She put her hand on the swell of his biceps before he could move away and guided him back to her desk. "It's all right." She slipped onto the seat, casually indicating the photos on-screen. "This is all for the video I'm putting together for Brian. It's already saved, so all we have to do is get out of this window, bring up the internet browser and then we can go shopping." Twenty minutes later, she and Nash had narrowed their search down to two possible items.

A green toy farm tractor Brian could sit on and pedal with his feet. It was sturdy and safe and just the right size. Or a yellow construction-style digger, with a dual action lever that could scoop up objects and move them elsewhere. It, too, was sturdy, and had a seat Brian could sit on. Instead of pedals, he would power it with his feet.

"I don't know." Callie bit her lip uncertainly, really needing a guy's opinion. Really needing Nash… She turned to him for help. "I can't decide. I think he would like both."

Straddling a ladder-back chair, Nash lifted his shoulders in a lazy shrug. "Why don't you get him one, and I'll get him the other?"

She studied his expression. "You really want to do that?"

His smile widened. "I was planning to get him a gift anyway, and this way, whenever Henry visits, both boys will have a 'tractor' to ride."

It did sound like the perfect solution.

Callie leaned across the expanse between them and kissed him on the cheek. "Thank you."

He caught her by the shoulders, returning the sweet caress. Finally, knowing as well as she that if they kept this up, they'd completely lose track of what they were supposed to be doing, he drew back. "Now, let's get these gifts ordered so they can be here by Monday at the latest."

Nodding, Callie turned back to the computer and began filling in the online form.

When she moved from billing information to shipping, Nash asked, "Would you like to have them delivered to my place—instead of yours?"

That would be so great. "Would you mind?"

"Not at all," he told her. "I'm glad to help out, as always."

Once the orders were confirmed, they went into the kitchen. Feeling genuinely festive, Callie turned on a Christmas CD. She was about to ask Nash if he wanted a dish of peppermint ice cream when he held a sprig of mistletoe above her head. Using his other arm to pull her close against him, he drawled, "Well, look here." He flashed a sexy grin. "How did that get in my pocket?"

NASH KNEW HE wasn't playing fair. Using their attraction for each other to draw Callie all the way into the present, but there were times, like now, when it was the best way to make her see that the past was over. There was no use hiding behind it, not when they had an emotional connection just as fierce as the chemistry between them. Not when he craved contact with her, craved…love.

Hooking the toe of his boot beneath the rung of a chair, he brought it all the way from the table and sank into it, dropping the mistletoe and pulling her onto his lap in the process. Gasping, she laughed in surprise as her bottom hit his thighs, and then all amusement faded as he kissed his way from temple to cheek, to the lobe of her ear, the hollow of her throat. "Nash…"

He drew back to see into her eyes, knowing he didn't need a cornball excuse to kiss her, touch her, hold her. "Kiss me, Callie…"

Wreathing her arms around his neck, she turned her head to his. Smiled with a devastating mix of tenderness and mischief. "Is that your Christmas wish?"

He grinned. "One of them."

Her answering laugh was soft, feminine, enticing. Rising slightly, she tugged the hem of her skirt to the top of her thighs, giving him quite the view and giving her maximum mobility. Blue eyes glittering, she swung one leg gracefully over his, then settled on his lap again, this time facing him.

His body roared to life.

"Like this?" she purred, all innocence, shifting her body over his in a way that let him know she was already every bit as turned on as he was.

"Exactly like this." Excitement rumbling through him, he waited to see what she was going to do.

She took his head in her hands, sifted her fingers through his hair and slowly, effortlessly lowered her mouth to his.

The first contact of her lips on his sent another jolt to

his system. Lower still, where she pressed against him, she was soft, hot…and damp.

Not at all sure he could control himself, he closed his eyes. Five minutes into the kiss, he was drowning in pleasure, kissing her back, devouring her mouth. Learning everything about her anew.

Needing more, he slid his hands beneath her cashmere sweater, found the front clasp of her bra. Her breasts came tumbling out. Wanting to watch her, to push her over the edge, he drew back, brought his hands to the outside of her sweater, then fit the cashmere fabric across her breasts, molding it to her soft curves. Her nipples poked against the fabric and she moaned. Smiling, he caressed her through the cloth, watching with pure delight as she began to tremble.

"Two can play at this game." She shifted again, rising slightly. She found the buckle on his belt, then his fly.

He caught her hand. "If mine come down, your tights and panties come *off.*"

She laughed again. Kept going until his pants and shorts were at midthigh. Then, her soft, delicate hands found and claimed him.

"Callie…" He throbbed beneath the tender, knowing ministrations of her hands.

"Eventually," she promised. "First, I want to…" She stroked her thumb from tip to base, over the rim, back down again, finding every sweet pleasurable inch. Kissing him all the while. The insides of her thighs moving back and forth over the outside of his, the friction of cloth to skin slowly but surely driving him insane.

His palms left her breasts. He tightened his grip on her hips. Making his own demands now, he moved his palms over her hips, pushing her skirt up around her waist, tugging the tights, then the panties down.

She broke off the kiss. Moved to let him peel them all the way off.

Then, skirt still on, she climbed astride his lap once again, making his every fantasy come true.

She lowered her head, and they kissed again, hotly, wantonly, lost in the moment. He stroked the inside of her thighs, the rounded curves of her buttocks, the taut silk of her lower abdomen, then tilted her in a way that pleased him. She moaned, shifting, writhing with pleasure. Knowing she was close, he touched her again, from the inside and out, as their breathing grew hot and heavy. She trembled, tried to hold back, as surely as he had. But it was too late. She could no longer deny him than he could deny her. He entered her as she came, pushing into her, filling her to the brim.

She whimpered in response and whispered his name.

Nothing had ever sounded so good or so right.

He brought her in closer still, feeling as if his heart was going to pound right out of his chest. Kissed her all the more deeply, the sensation of being locked inside her, rocking his world.

Hers, too, he thought in satisfaction, if her erratic breathing and wild, abandoned kisses were any indication. He slowed and erotically shifted his angle, aware that making love with her was the most amazing thing he had ever experienced. And then there was no more thinking, only feeling. No more holding back. Only letting go. And together they soared into the sweetest, hottest pleasure either of them had ever known.

CALLIE COLLAPSED AGAINST NASH, every single cell in her body tingling. Sated. She was still throbbing with the force of her orgasm and yet she wanted him again. Wanted him so bad her toes curled. How wild was that?

No wilder than the feelings she was beginning to have for him.

No wilder than the thought that she might—just might—be on the verge of falling—

No, she couldn't think that way. Wouldn't let herself think that way. What they had now was good enough to get them through the holidays and more. Once the sentimental time had passed, life would go back to normal. And with that, would come the normalization of her feelings, too. She'd stop feeling like her life wasn't right without him in it. She wouldn't feel so restless. So in need of a man. Of marriage and a complete family. So in need of Nash…

As if reading her thoughts, Nash ran a hand up and down her back in a way that felt so good she nearly moaned. "Want to go upstairs?" He brushed a kiss against her ear.

She did. More than he would ever know. She also knew relying on someone else to that degree again was not wise. She'd barely survived her first loss, and she hadn't felt anywhere near as passionately about Seth as she did about Nash.

Tamping down the need welling inside her heart, she returned his tender smile with a playful one of her own. "You know if we do, we won't get any sleep at all tonight." She stroked her hand through his thick black hair. "And with the big celebration tomorrow…"

Once again, he understood her with the patience of a saint. "We both need to be on our A game."

"Plus—" Callie drew a deep breath. Knowing this had to be said so the possibility wouldn't come up again, she sat up straight. "You see how much Brian talks. If my son were to find you here in the morning, and real-ize you'd spent the night…" *In my bed*. He'd know how real and right this all was.

He'd want and expect it to happen more.

And so would I.

Nash kissed the inside of her wrist, finishing her thought. "Everyone would know."

Callie trembled at his evocative touch. Lower still, where she straddled him, she could feel the resurgence of his desire. And hers. Doing her best to keep her mind on the topic at hand, she said, "Preschool pals. Teachers. Friends. Family…"

Nash looked deep into her eyes. He traced her lower lip with the pad of his thumb, his touch on her calming. "Which is not what you want."

Callie luxuriated in his warmth and understanding. Was there anything she did not love about this man? "If I ever have a man stay the night, I want it to be because we're married. And I'm not sure I want to be married again." She studied his reaction. "Does that sound hope-lessly old-fashioned?"

Nash brought her close and kissed her tenderly. "It sounds," he murmured huskily, "exactly like you."

"Trouble?" Nash asked the next morning when he ar-rived to pick up Callie and Brian. He'd left the night be-fore—reluctantly—but the good night's sleep was worth it today.

Callie was looking absolutely gorgeous in a red-and-black taffeta striped gown. The high-collared, long-sleeved dress clung to her breasts and waist before flaring out at her hips and swirling elegantly to the floor. It rustled when she walked.

Unfortunately, despite her well-rested appearance, her day appeared not to be starting off as smoothly as she had hoped.

Callie sighed with frustration. "Brian doesn't like his vintage clothing. I'm hoping you can help."

Nash hoped so, too, since they were due at the Double Knot Ranch in fifteen minutes. He walked into the family room and carefully scoped out the situation. Brian was lying prone on the floor, his expression mulish. Nash knelt down to greet the tantrum-throwing little boy. "What's the problem, buddy?" he inquired matter-of-factly. As if this were something he dealt with every day.

Brian plucked at his charcoal tweed knickers and kicked his legs like a bucking donkey. Callie had managed to get a white T-shirt on him, too, but that was all. The black knee socks he was supposed to wear had been hurled off to the side. Ditto the lace-up black shoes, tweed newsboy cap, matching jacket, red bow tie and white shirt.

"Don't. Like." Each word was accompanied by another donkey-like kick of the legs.

Nash arrowed a hand at his chest, demonstrating. "Hey, I'm dressed up, too."

Brian turned his head. He surveyed Nash's dark Western suit, finely pressed shirt, red-and-gold brocade vest, matching tie and black Stetson.

"Everybody has to get dressed up to see Santa Claus today," Nash explained.

At the mention of Old St. Nick, Brian's eyes lit up.

Nash continued using the carrot-and-stick approach. "I know you want to see the North Pole and sit on Santa's

lap so you can tell him what you want for Christmas."
While he talked, Nash gathered up the clothes.

"And besides," he pointed out gently, easing Brian to
a sitting position, "our shirts match. See? Mine is white,
and it has buttons up the front. And yours is white and
has buttons up the front, too. It's a big-boy shirt."

Mollified, Brian held out his arms so Nash could ease
them into the sleeves.

"You—Santa—too?" Brian asked.

Nash grinned as he helped Brian put on his socks
and shoes. "I think I'm too big to sit on Santa's lap." He
made a comical face, eliciting a giggle from the child. "I
might *squish* him. And then what would we do? If Santa
was all *squished*?"

Brian giggled some more.

On went the jacket. The snap on tie. The cap.

Callie hovered nearby, chuckling, too.

"There," Nash said, arms waving with dramatic flourish. "You're looking good, buddy. And just like me." He
turned to Callie, "Okay, Mommy, I believe we're good
to go. What do you say we take our picture before hitting the road?"

Callie got out her phone, aiming at Nash and Brian.

Nash motioned her closer. "I meant all three of us."

Grinning, Callie rustled closer. Nash picked Brian
up, clasped him against his chest, then put his other arm
around Callie. She held out the phone. And the first selfie
of their relationship was taken.

Chapter Fourteen

Although the Old-Fashioned Christmas Celebration would not begin for another hour, the 1880s Western-garbed waitstaff was already busy setting up a sumptuous holiday buffet when Callie, Brian and Nash walked in to the party barn. Admiring the festive decor, she smiled with relief that all their hard work and planning had truly paid off.

In one corner, children's arts and crafts tables were situated. Santa's village occupied another corner. Musicians were tuning up on stage. Beautifully adorned gift baskets for the guests were being laid out. Gifts for the door prizes—handmade candles, quilts, cakes, Christmas trees and wreaths—were also on display. Along with the brochures that Callie had made for the local businesses sponsoring the event.

She settled her son with the other kids being supervised by local art students, then went to work setting up, too, while Nash assisted with some of the heavy lifting. "You look happy," Maggie said, when she caught up with her.

Callie returned her twin's hug. "And you don't." She paused. "What's wrong?"

Maggie frowned. "It's Hart. He's got the flu."

Callie sympathized. "Oh, no."

"He went to the urgent care clinic first thing this morning, and got started on antiviral medicine, which should limit it, but he's not going to be able to be—" Maggie paused as a couple of children passed by "—You Know Who today. And we got the, um, You Know What to fit him. So…" Maggie waved Nash over then paused to size him up with a critical eye. "You're about the same size. Six foot four, give or take, two hundred and twenty pounds…"

Of pure solid muscle, Callie added silently. *A very sexual being. Kind, loving, funny, charming. Intelligent. And so much more…*

Oblivious to her adoring thoughts, Nash asked, "Need a volunteer?"

Maggie shot him a grateful glance. "Pronto. So, if you wouldn't mind… Callie can you help him? The costume is in the main house, in one of the upstairs bedrooms. You can't miss it. When you're ready, let us know, and we'll set up for your 'big entrance.'"

"And here I was just getting used to your Texas Maverick look," Callie quipped, picking up her skirts and leading the way as she and Nash slipped out of the party barn and headed across the lawn.

On the other side of the parking lot, the steam engine warmed up beside the train station, preparing for the run up to the mountaintop and Nature's Cathedral, where an outdoor concert would be held every hour on the hour. Overhead, the skies were still a wintry gray, but perhaps that wasn't such a bad thing given it was a Christmas celebration. Had it been sunny and seventy degrees, it would have been a lot harder to get in the mood.

Playful as ever, Nash winked. "I can put it all back on

later, if you like. In fact, I'm going to have to—unless you want me to go home au naturel."

Callie snickered. "Cute. And no, G-rated is fine." They moved inside the house, out of sight of others. "This is a family event. Remember?"

As soon as the words were out, she regretted them. "Oh, Nash, I'm sorry," she breathed, embarrassed.

"Don't be," Nash returned gruffly. He leaned in and kissed her cheek. "I've got lots of friends."

"But—"

He tightened his grip on her. "Right now you and Brian are the only family I need."

To her surprise, as she luxuriated in the feel of his strong arms around her, Callie felt the same.

It was easy to tell which room was designated as Santa's dressing room. There was a cutout sleigh taped to the shut door. Callie knocked, just to be on the safe side. When there was no answer, they slipped on in. "You may need a little help adjusting the padding."

Nash flashed her a sly grin. "No volunteer I'd rather have." He shucked the gambler clothing in no time flat.

Doing her best to keep her mind on the business at hand, which wasn't easy given his mouthwateringly fit physique, she handed him the red fleece pants then went to retrieve the black knee high boots.

"Have you ever done this before?" she felt compelled to ask.

Nash deliberately misinterpreted her question. "Taken off my clothes in front of you? Why, yes, ma'am." He tipped an imaginary hat and strolled closer still, crisp white T-shirt clinging magnificently to his bare chest and broad shoulders. "I have." His glance roved her up and down, lingering on each and every sensitive spot. "I have to admit I enjoyed it, too."

She batted his mischievously roaming hands away and fought back the desire to kiss him. "I meant played Santa."

"No." He pulled her closer still, his hands sliding down her waist to her hips. He fitted her against him— at least as much as her full skirt and his loose-fitting trousers would allow. "Can't say that I have."

A thrill swept through her as she felt his hardness and the answering tingle within her body. Extricating herself, she went to get the padding that would give him the girth he needed to play Old St. Nick. With him watching her closely, she adjusted the elastic straps over his shoulders and around his waist, situating the pillow where his belly should be.

"I could get used to this," he drawled.

So could she. Whoever would have thought playing dress-up with the man she lo—lusted after—could be so much fun? Doing her best to keep her feelings in check, she batted her lashes at him flirtatiously. "Ho, ho, Santa."

His low laugh filled the room as she tugged the suspenders holding his pants up over his broad shoulders. The red coat with the white fur trim followed. He sat down on the edge of the bed so she could properly situate the curly white wig, mustache and beard. Still standing between his spread thighs, she planted the hat on his head and then stepped back slightly to admire her handiwork.

"Sexy Texas maverick to old man in three minutes. Not bad."

Nash vaulted to his feet, unabashed desire in his eyes. He wrapped his hands around her waist and guided her close. When she was snug against him, he tugged down the beard, lowered his head and delivered a long, hot, scintillating kiss that rocked her world.

When he finally released her, she was trembling all over. Wanting him so much it hurt.

He winked. "Consider that a down payment for later."

"I*F* I DIDN'T know better," Maggie remarked after Callie had returned to the party barn alone, "I'd think you'd been making out." She paused, cookie tray in hand, and looked closer. "You *have* been making out!"

Callie struggled not to blush and busied herself filling bowls with individually wrapped chocolate peppermint candies. "Shush."

"Hmm. Well, at least one of us is getting a little yuletide action," Maggie teased dryly, looking genuinely happy for her sister.

Then she sighed abruptly, her expression becoming fretful once again.

Callie sympathized, "Worried about Hart?"

Maggie set a row of snowball cookies next to the gingersnaps. "It is so hard to keep that man in bed," she lamented.

Callie snorted.

Maggie suppressed a laugh at the accidental double entendre. "*Resting*, I mean. You know these big tough guys. They hate being sick."

"And hate following doctor's orders even more?" Callie guessed.

"Exactly."

And getting extra sleep was the fastest way to recovery from any illness, they both knew. "So rest with him," Callie suggested, as they headed back to the kitchen, empty trays in hand. "I mean it. You've kept Brian for me several times recently. Why not let me reciprocate this evening with Henry?"

Her twin offered a faint smile. "Only one problem with that. Frank and Fiona have already called dibs on him." And grandparents ruled, that Callie knew. "But," her twin continued, hopefully, "if you wanted to have Henry over to play with Brian tomorrow…"

"Consider it done," Callie vowed with a hug.

No sooner had they deposited their trays and returned to the party, than the music struck up. "Jingle Bells! Jingle Bells! Jingle all the way…"

All eyes turned, as Santa strode into the party barn, a big sack of toys slung over one brawny shoulder. "Ho, Ho, Ho! Merry Christmas!" Nash said in a deep and rumbling voice that sounded nothing like his usual Texas drawl.

"And here we go." Maggie beamed.

Together, she and Callie rounded up the children congregated in the arts and crafts area of the party barn, and took them over to see Santa, one by one.

Henry did great. As did all the other children. Finally, it was Brian's turn.

Callie led him over to the North Pole. His normal bashfulness in such situations absent—maybe because so many kids had already gone ahead of him—Brian climbed importantly up onto Santa's lap, an inquisitive look in his baby-blue eyes.

Oh, no, Callie thought. *Please tell me he's not going to ask Santa if* he *is his daddy?* And for a second, that was exactly what she thought her son was going to say.

Instead, Brian stared at Santa long and hard. Putting

both his hands on Santa's bearded cheeks, Brian stared deep into his eyes.

Santa looked back, kindly, lovingly.

Callie could not tell whether or not her son recognized Nash, but he definitely sensed some sort of connection.

"Well, hello there, young man," Nash said in an impressively well-disguised baritone. "Have you been a good boy this year? Helped your mommy out? Picked up your toys and gone to bed on time?"

Brian had to think about that. Finally, he nodded soberly. "That's good to hear," Santa said, quietly and authoritatively. "What would you like me to bring you for Christmas?"

Again, Callie held her breath.

And Brian said, "My friend Nash."

NASH HAD PREPARED himself for many things. The request for a daddy, for instance. Or being recognized, his identity blown.

But never this.

Sensing Nash just wasn't getting what he meant, Brian added, "Stay—me."

"You want Nash to stay with you?" he asked.

Brian nodded soberly. "Stay—Mommy, too."

"Oh. Well…" Nash worked to stay in character "…that's not the kind of thing Santa and his elves can bring you." But it was the sort of thing *he* could work on. "Santa can bring you toys, though." He stroked his beard thoughtfully. "So, young man, what would you like Santa to bring you that you can play with?"

Again, Brian had to think. He settled back down again, leaning against the curve of "Santa's" big, strong arm as he gave the question careful consideration.

"A puppy," he said at last.

Beside them, Callie nearly fell through the floor.

Figuring he should quit while he was ahead, Nash said, "All right then, Brian. Let's get your picture taken with Santa. Mommy, you can be in the photo, too, if you like, and then you'll be good to go…"

Just that quickly, the visit was concluded, and Brian scrambled off Nash's lap. After one long last thoughtful look back at him, the two-and-a-half-year-old went off to ride the steam engine with his mother and a whole host of other parents and children.

Nash continued to be Santa for several more hours.

He left with the same flourish he'd entered the party barn with, then slipped off to change back into his Western garb to hand out the free Christmas trees and wreaths—on behalf of his business—to departing guests. Meanwhile, Callie was in charge of presenting the gift baskets to all the adults, and Maggie had the goodie bags for the kids.

The incredibly successful day ended with a private celebratory dinner for everyone who had worked the event. It was a lively affair, and by the time Callie and Nash returned to her ranch, still in costume, Brian was already sound asleep.

Callie tucked her son into bed, then returned with a bottle of champagne and two glasses. The cold winter rain that had been predicted began to fall, and they settled before the fire and began discussing the day.

"It could have been worse," Nash told Callie, when talk turned to Brian's visit with Santa. "He could have asked for a sibling. In fact, he probably will once Maggie has her baby and his cousin Henry has a little brother or sister."

Callie groaned and then buried her face in her hands. "Let's not jump ahead of ourselves. Let's focus instead on what we're going to do about the puppy situation."

Nash liked the way she was including him in the decision-making process—as if he were truly part of her immediate family now. He also liked the way she looked in that vintage red-and-black-striped taffeta gown—*and* the fact that she hadn't taken it off yet. Because he had been fantasizing about doing just that, all day long…

Callie handed him the bottle. He loosened the wire cage holding the cork in place and then, holding the bottle forty-five degrees away from them, opened it carefully. "Are you ready for a little four-legged critter?" He poured while she held the glasses.

Callie hesitated. "When Brian is older, yes. Not now."

Nash toasted her with a smile, then clinked his glass against hers.

"I might be."

She studied him. "Seriously?"

Nash shrugged, admitting, "It gets a little lonely at the ranch. I wouldn't mind some company." *I wouldn't mind having you and Brian there*. But he knew that was the kind of overly romantic declaration she didn't want to hear. Not yet, anyway. "But we digress," he said, taking her free hand in his.

"Yes." Sighing softly, Callie shifted around so she was nestled in the curve of his body, her head resting on his shoulder. "We do."

Enjoying their closeness, he leaned down to breathe in the fragrant flowery scent of her hair. "How about I pick up a stuffed toy puppy for him?" He pressed a kiss against her temple. "I have to go into San Antonio tomorrow anyway." *To get a present for you.* "I could get one for Santa to bring him then."

She shifted again, her thigh bumping against his, causing his body to harden. "You wouldn't mind?"

Nash took another sip of the chilled champagne. "Not at all." He set his glass aside, relieved her of hers, too. Standing, he took her by the hand, drew her to her feet. "Of course," he teased, retrieving both glasses and bottle of bubbly before leading her mischievously toward the stairs, "I am going to need payment for my trouble."

She accompanied him down the hall, stopping to kiss him every five or six steps. Eventually, they ended up in her bedroom. She locked the door behind them, pausing to turn on the bedside lamp, then sashayed toward him. Her blue eyes as mischievous as her voice, she watched him put the champagne aside for later, then asked, "What kind of payment?"

What kind indeed? "Hmm…" Nash pretended to think as she came to a halt in front of him. He bent and kissed the side of her neck, felt her arch pliantly against him. "I have been wanting to try to get you out of this dress all day—or see what was required to get you out of this dress."

She batted her lashes in all innocence. "And leave my virtue intact?"

He laughed, loving the playful, womanly side of her. "No one said anything about virtue…" he teased, unbuttoning one fitted sleeve from wrist to forearm. Then the other.

She trembled when he reached for the row of buttons that stretched from the high-banded collar to just below her waist.

One by one, he undid them, opening up the cloth at

her throat, past the ridges of her breasts, her ribs, all the way to her waist. Finished, he parted the cloth. "No modern-day garment this," he breathed.

It was sexy as hell. Made of some sort of soft, delicate, nearly transparent linen. Laced snugly up the front. Her breasts spilling over the lace-edged décolletage…

He hardened just looking at the imprint of her rose-colored nipples pressing against the cloth.

A tug and the top of her dress slithered to her waist. Another shift and the skirt pushed past her hips, fell to a circle on the floor.

However, to his chagrin, the sexy-as-hell chemise disappeared into another floor-length slip-style thing. "What's this?" he asked.

"Petticoat."

"How do I get it off?"

She turned, offering him her back. "Untie it."

He did, but upon pushing it off, found the chemise only went to midthigh. "Anything beneath *this*?" he asked huskily.

She wreathed her arms about his neck. Looked him in the eye. Smiled coyly. "Find out."

He slipped his hands over her thighs, slid them upward, encountered…the one modern-day garment she had on. Tiny red silk bikini panties. "These I am familiar with."

Another smile. "No way was I wearing pantaloons."

"Can't blame you. Although—" he went back to unlacing the front of her chemise "—I do like this."

"I thought you might."

He opened up the edges. Her breasts spilled out. The curves round and silky and pale. The nipples jutting proudly. He covered them with his hands, felt them press into his palms. He lowered his head to hers. She shuddered in response as he kissed her. Her eyes drifted closed, even as her hand slid between them and went to the buttons on his vest. Then his shirt. He shrugged out of both, still kissing her, then spread the edges of her chemise so her breasts were crushed against his bare chest.

She moaned, her body responding to the friction of their skin. Lower still, she was damp, trembling. He eased his hand beneath the elastic of her panties, touching, caressing, tempting, teasing. She reached for the belt of his pants. He caught her hands and held them behind her. Turned her so her back was to his front, then let his free hand slide lower to find the softness.

She whimpered as he slid his palm over her mound, tracing the flowering petals with his fingertips, easing his way inside. Again, and then again. And again. "Nash…"

"Open for me, Callie. All the way. Show me how much you want me…"

She sagged against him, knees weakening, trembling, coming apart in his hands. And again he touched her. Finding. Soothing. Stroking. Until there was no more waiting. Only wanting.

He turned her so she was facing him. Eased her back against the wall. Swiftly disrobed. Loving the sight of her, clad in nothing but the filmy chemise, body aching with the need to claim her, he stepped between her spread thighs.

Breathing raggedly, he lifted her until she was at just the right height. Feeling her full voluptuous breasts tautening, her whole body quivering, his pleasure intensified threefold as her naked thighs brushed against his. Welcoming him home into her silky softness, she tangled her hands in his hair, forcing his mouth back to hers, kissing him until he felt his soul stripped bare. His head got a little lighter, his body got harder. And still they claimed each other. Kissing again and again and again. Moving together. Ever higher. Loving each other with everything they had. Until at last, there was no more holding back, no more waiting, nothing but the most incredible pleasure. And the exaltation of their hearts.

And Nash knew the Christmas he had been longing for, the meaning he had coveted, was finally here.

Chapter Fifteen

Nash was headed out the door of his ranch house the following morning, when his phone rang. "Hey, Nash, it's Fiona Sanders. I was just checking to see if you had made a decision about our open house on Christmas Day."

Nash checked his pocket to make sure he had his wallet. "When did you need to know?"

"Got a better invitation?" she teased, clearly in matchmaker mode.

No, but he was hoping for one. "Actually," Nash said honestly, "this year I've had a half-dozen invitations for both Christmas Day and Christmas Eve." Seemed as if now that he was back for good, everyone was trying to fix him up.

"So you haven't made up your mind, in other words," the older woman guessed.

"I'm not sure if I want to try to hit every gathering— at least for a little while—or just spend the time at home, chilling out." And missing Callie and Brian, who were both due to be in her hometown of Laramie, Texas, on December twenty-fourth and twenty-fifth.

Fiona paused, understanding as always. "Just know you are always welcome in our home. You always have been."

Gratitude welled in his throat. In many ways, Hart's mom had taken the place of his own, in his life, since his parents had moved to Japan. Looking out for him, always making sure he was doing okay, the way any mom of an adult son would. "Thanks, Fiona."

"So what's on your agenda today?" Fiona asked cheerfully.

"Every man's favorite thing—shopping." He had a lot of gift buying to do, and given it was now December twenty-first, not a lot of time left to do it.

THE RAIN WAS still coming down in droves when Maggie arrived at Callie's home at midmorning, little Henry in tow. After hearing that Hart was definitely on the mend and would be well in time to celebrate the holiday, Callie asked, "Mind looking at something for me?"

"Sure." Maggie left the boys playing with blocks and followed Callie into the living room.

"This morning, the video-guy sent me the finished compilation of the DVD I made for Brian about Seth. Want to tell me what you think?"

Maggie sat down in front of the computer and hit Play. The volume was adjusted to low, but an orchestral version of an upbeat Disney tune could be heard in the background of the five-minute video that tracked Seth from early adulthood to his courtship with Callie to their wedding day and subsequent move into their first place. Sadly, there was nothing after that to showcase.

"Looks good," Maggie said approvingly. "But clearly something is bothering you."

Callie swallowed, trying to get ahold of herself. "I put a rush on this because I wanted to have it ready in time for Christmas, in case there were any issues with not having a male parent around."

"And now?" her twin asked gently.

"Brian's been so happy lately."

"Because of Nash?"

Callie nodded, feeling happy that this was the case—and, at the same time, a little worried it wouldn't last. That something unforeseen would happen to her and Nash, too...

Maggie stepped away from the computer. Fondly, she recollected, "That was something yesterday, what Brian asked Santa to bring him—and you—for Christmas."

Callie blushed, aware how much she wanted the same thing. Nash—for Christmas. "I know." She walked into the kitchen and set the teakettle on to boil.

"My only question is, what are you going to do about it?" Maggie lounged against the counter. "Have you even bought him a gift?"

Sort of. "You know how I had Brian make everyone a gift this year?"

Maggie nodded.

Callie got out the tea and all the fixin's. "I was thinking about doing something along those lines for Nash, too."

"Sounds good," her twin encouraged.

The question was, Callie thought, would Nash think so, too?

SHE FOUND OUT when he stopped by later that evening. Brian, tired from a whole day of playing with his cousin Henry, was already upstairs, fast asleep. Nash was dressed casually like her—in jeans and a sweater. With raindrops glinting in his thick dark hair, his cheeks ruddy with cold, he was sexy as all get-out. Their gazes met and held, and deep inside her, desire built.

"How did the shopping go?" Callie asked, ushering him inside.

He hung up his coat, and taking her hand in his, gave it a squeeze. "Good. Finally. I think… I hope."

Deciding she wanted more, she turned around to give him a full-body hug. He returned it in spades and followed it with a long, leisurely kiss that kicked up her pulse even more.

"I guess we'll find out soon," Nash added humorously.

"You sound like you have my talent when it comes to gift giving," Callie teased. She wrinkled her nose at him.

"A whole lot of thought without necessarily reaping a whole lot of result?" Nash paraphrased.

She laughed and drew him into the living room to sit before the fire. "And the more pressure there is to come up with the perfect gift, the more unpredictable the result."

"Pretty much, yeah. Although," he boasted as he settled next to her on the sofa, "I think I may have nailed it with you."

Which made it even more important that he like what she wanted to give to him. Sobering, Callie cleared her throat and took both of his hands in hers. "Speaking of presents, I want to talk to you about the one I am proposing that Brian and I give you."

"Okay."

She struggled with a myriad of emotions. "You know that I'm supposed to drive Brian home to Laramie on December 24 and spend Christmas Eve with my in-laws, and Christmas Day with my family. It's tradition. And I'm really looking forward to it." She tightened her fingers on his. "But I really wanted to spend Christmas with you, too."

He gazed into her eyes and returned softly, "I've been thinking about that, too. Because I really want to enjoy the holiday with you and Brian."

"So here's what I propose. What if tomorrow night, you and I create our own Christmas Eve celebration here, and then have our own Christmas Day celebration together early on December 24? Before I head to Laramie with Brian."

He lifted a shoulder. "Or I could go with the two of you to your hometown and enjoy Christmas with you there." He paused. "Seems like it might be easier for you and less confusing for Brian. Although I would also like to be with you on the twenty-third. So we could still do our own private celebration before we left."

Callie bit her lip, wondering how everything could go awry so quickly. "You want to meet my parents?" she asked in shock, not sure she was anywhere near ready for that.

"And all your sisters." Nash flashed another easy half smile. "I've already met Doris and Rock."

Her emotions in turmoil, Callie withdrew her hands, stood. Outside the rain continued to fall, harder now. Unable to look into his eyes, she paced away from Nash. "That's not a good idea."

He followed her to the hearth. "Why not?"

She whirled to face him. "Because if I were to take you home it would be a whole different holiday than the one I have planned."

His face took on a brooding expression. "In what way?"

"You know how wildly enthusiastic Doris and Rock

are, under the best of circumstances. They already have us practically married off. So if I were to just show up with you on my arm, they would take it to mean we were as serious about each other as they had hoped." She winced. "And then they'd be shouting it from the rooftops to everyone in town."

Tension knotted her gut as she forced herself to continue as pragmatically as possible. "And, on the other end of the spectrum, we'd have my parents jumping to the same conclusion as Rock and Doris." She paused to look Nash in the eye, and her throat ached with the tears she suppressed.

"Only my folks wouldn't approve, Nash." She moved closer. "Because the last thing they want to see is me diving into something heart-first, when I've already made that mistake once before."

He regarded her soberly, still listening.

"And then there's my son to consider. You've heard him, Nash! He already wants you to come and live with us. If I take you home to Laramie, and everyone reacts the way I predict, Brian will be elated when he's around Doris and Rock, and even more confused and upset when he's around my parents." She sighed wearily. "It would just be a bad situation, all around."

He folded his arms across his chest. "And of course that's not what you want."

His accusation stung. Again, she tried to make him understand. "I just want things to stay simple, and easy, and uncomplicated." Even though that didn't really seem possible, especially when her feelings for Nash were so complicated. And getting more so every day. "At least whenever I'm in Laramie," Callie added lamely.

"Where you are still known as the tragic young

widow." He lifted a hand before she could protest. "Those are your words, Callie, not mine."

She lifted her chin. "I don't like being referred to that way!" It was a miserable way to live. And he knew it, too—since he had suffered a similar fate due to his own family tragedy.

He continued to study her calmly. "Then why not do something to change it?"

Irked by his refusal to understand, Callie threw up her hands. "I have. I moved away. I struck out on my own." All of that had helped her cast off the stigma of being a young widow. "And that's where I would like to keep things for now."

"Meaning what?" he countered. "You don't want any man in your life—at least publicly? It's okay if we have an affair in the shadows, as long as no one else knows about it? Is that what the deal is?"

Pretty much. "For now. However, in the future," Callie promised sincerely, when she felt she could handle it, "things will be different."

Cynicism darkened his slate-gray eyes. "Okay. Give me a timetable. If not now, when will you let people know that you and I are seeing each other? *Seriously* seeing each other?"

"I—"

He stood his ground. "January? February? March? Six months from now? A year?"

"I don't know. Whenever it feels right!"

He exhaled roughly, looking as ticked off as she felt. "Or maybe never."

An ugly silence fell. To the point Callie wondered if she had ever really known him at all.

"Why are you putting all this pressure on me?" she asked, upset.

His jaw clenching, he braced himself as if for battle. "Because you aren't the only one who doesn't want to make the same mistakes you made before," he said in a low, accusing tone. "Because I spent the last half of my childhood pinning my hopes on my parents' promise that one day they would get over my brother's death, that one day things would be normal again, that one day we'd be able to celebrate Christmas and treasure all that we still had, instead of dwelling on what we had lost."

He moved closer, pain radiating in his eyes and voice. She could swear she saw the glimmer of tears. "Only it never happened, Callie. Those were empty promises given by two people who had either forgotten—or maybe were just unwilling—to ever fill their lives with love again."

Now she was crying, too. "I'm not like that."

His glance raked over her sadly. "You just don't want to ever marry again."

Feeling as if her whole world was crashing down upon her once again, she moved closer, locking her eyes with his. "I was honest with you about that from the very first," she reminded him quietly. Before he had come into her life, she hadn't thought she could ever risk it. She still wasn't sure she could.

Nash's shoulders sagged in defeat. "You're right—you were up front about that," he admitted. "I just didn't listen." He gave her one long, last look, then said quietly, "Merry Christmas, Callie. Tell Brian I wish him the same."

He grabbed his coat, and without a backward glance, walked out into the icy December rain.

Chapter Sixteen

"Well, there you are!" the jeweler said. "We didn't think you were ever going to come in to pick up your rings."

Callie forced a smile she couldn't begin to feel as she handed over her credit card for payment. "I'm sorry it's taken me so long."

"Busy time?" The kind older man gave her the slip to sign, then went to retrieve her jewelry.

"Very," Callie told him when he returned. At least it had been. Now, with Nash out of her life, things seemed lonely. Quiet. Too quiet.

The jeweler put the engagement and wedding rings out for Callie to inspect. "How do they look?"

"Beautiful," Callie said softly. The platinum bands gleamed and the diamond sparkled radiantly—yet seemed like a lifetime ago, too.

"Would you like to wear them out?" the jeweler asked.

Callie knew her days of wearing her rings and pretending she was still married—even if it was just to discourage men from approaching her—were over. "I'll carry them, thanks."

The jeweler tucked her rings into the satin folds of a small velvet box. He closed it and slid it into a bag. "Have a merry Christmas!" he said.

"You, too," Callie replied. Although inwardly, it was hard to imagine how she was going to be very merry without Nash in her life. But like it or not, she had to move on.

So Callie went to the bank. She placed her rings in her safety deposit box, along with all the other important papers relating to her marriage to Seth. Then headed to her sister's to pick up Brian, who was happily playing "Reindeer and Santa Claus" with his cousin Henry in the family room while Maggie wrapped presents for the extended family nearby.

Callie made herself a cup of peppermint tea and sat down. "Where's Hart?"

"Out doing stuff for Christmas."

Glad to turn the spotlight on someone else, she said playfully, "Don't tell me he's a last-minute shopper."

"Are you kidding?" Maggie fit a blender on the wrapping paper, then began to cut it to the appropriate size. "He took care of all that weeks ago. He's on a more personal mission today, and don't ask me anything more, because that's all I know. And speaking of being kept in the dark…" She taped the paper into place. "You want to tell me what's going on with you and Nash? Brian told Henry that you were sad last night."

Callie tensed. "He wasn't supposed to know that." In fact, still determined to give her son the best Christmas ever, she had done her best to put on a merry front for her little boy's behalf.

Maggie affixed a big bow to the package. "Well, obviously, he picked up on your mood anyway." She paused to give her twin a pointed look. "So what's going on?"

Briefly, Callie brought her sister up to speed. When she'd finished, silence fell between them. Maggie reached for another gift. "Do you still think you made the right decision?" she asked quietly.

Callie helped her sister center the present on the paper, then handed her the scissors. "I can't take Nash home to Laramie with me, Maggie. Not at this point, anyway. It's hard enough for me to get through the holidays, as is."

Her sister folded the ends into neat triangular shapes and taped them against the seam. "You don't think Nash would make it all easier for you?"

Callie swallowed her tea with a grimace. "Here at the ranch with just me and Brian? Yes. Back in Laramie, with Seth's parents trying to get me to marry again as soon as possible, and Mom and Dad trying to keep me from rushing into anything heart-first? No."

"Come on, Callie. You can handle parental meddling. You always have."

She shrugged. "So?"

Maggie gave her another look that saw way too much. "There's more to your not wanting to take Nash home with you than what you've said thus far. And don't tell me it's gossip from the locals, either, because even if you don't like it, you can handle that, too."

Knowing it would be cathartic to unburden herself to her twin, Callie sighed. "I'm in a good place now, Maggie. At least I have been, up until yesterday." She traced the handle on the tea mug, then took another sip. "And you know why I've been feeling so strong and together?" Deciding the tea tasted way too bitter, she got up and rummaged around for some sugar. "Because I've maintained my independence and kept everything in perspective."

Maggie finished another present and set it aside. She got up to make herself a cup of tea, too. Suddenly they heard whoops came from the family room, then the jingle of bells and more hearty ho-ho-hos. Mugs in hand, Maggie and Callie peeked around the corner. The boys were seated side by side on the sofa, pretending to drive the sleigh.

Grinning, the twins returned to the gift-wrapping and their unresolved conversation. "Look, I'm the first to admit you've been doing great, Callie. And yet, there's been something vital missing from your life. Even Brian—as young as he is—feels it."

"Hey, I do a great job as a single mom."

"No one said you didn't," Maggie returned gently. "But there's more to life than putting a moat around your heart. More to teach your son, too." She paused to let her words sink in. "Especially at this time of year."

Guilt flooded her. She knew Christmas was about giving, and that Nash had been giving a lot more than he had been taking, and she had been taking a lot more than she had been giving. She had hoped to rectify that by giving him the happy family Christmas he'd been longing for—a day early—but he'd rejected that as too little. Not realizing what it had cost her to stop protecting herself and her son to even offer that. And now the two of them were at a stalemate. Feeling like more of a failure than ever, Callie sighed again. "Look, Maggie, I know your life is more wonderful than you ever dreamed it could be. And it's all because of the joy Hart brought to your life."

"He taught me to lower my guard and put myself out there." Maggie hesitated. "It seems to me that Nash is doing the same for you. Or trying."

"I know that." Callie felt on the verge of crying once

again. She was never as happy as she was with him. The same went for her son.

"But?"

She blinked back her tears. "Everything was moving too fast."

"Sometimes life does."

Fear gripped her heart. "I can't go back to living in a cloud of romance."

Her twin shook her head at her in exasperation. "As opposed to a cloud of despair?"

Callie dug in stubbornly. "I have Brian to think of now. I can't afford to fall apart again, the way I did after Seth died."

"You're talking about your bout of exhaustion," Maggie guessed.

Callie nodded miserably. "If I hadn't allowed myself to wrap my whole life around Seth, if I had maintained at least some emotional independence, then I would have fared a whole lot better after his death."

"Oh, Callie." Maggie's own eyes filled with tears as she took her sister in her arms and hugged her fiercely, understanding as only an identical twin could. "It wasn't that you felt too much, it was what you refused to allow yourself to feel that sent you reeling."

Was her sister right? Callie wondered in shock. Was that really the case?

She wondered about it all the way home. By the time they reached the ranch, her son had taken on her low, dispirited mood. Thinking maybe this was the time to show him the comforting video montage of his father she had made, she popped the DVD in and sat down with him on the sofa.

He watched the five-minute video of Seth, which had

been set to some of his favorite upbeat music, with quiet fascination. Heartened by his positive response, Maggie turned to him and said, "Again?"

Brian nodded.

He watched it again, still thoughtful. Then, when it had ended, turned to her and asked, "Where my friend, Mommy?" Brian's lower lip quavered and his blue eyes were so sad they broke her heart. "Where Nash?"

LATE ON THE afternoon of December 22, Nash opened the front door. He took one look at Hart's face and knew the word had spread. "You heard."

Hart stepped inside the ranch house, his expression grim but determined. "Maggie told me. And for the record, I think you're making a terrible mistake letting Callie push you away."

Nash shrugged. "It's not like I have much choice."

"There's always a choice," his friend said.

"I'm looking for someone who's in it for the long haul. She doesn't want to get married, any more than my ex did."

Hart slid him a sly look. "You're that bad of a catch?"

Nash poked at the fire in the hearth. "It doesn't have anything to do with me."

"Sure about that?"

He shifted the logs until the flames leaped once again. "It has to do with the fact she's still mourning the loss of Seth and may never be ready or able to move on."

Hart lounged against the mantel and folded his arms across his chest. "She seemed over him to me. To Maggie, too."

Nash released a short, mirthless laugh. "She was still wearing her wedding rings a month ago."

"She's not wearing them now."

Nash replaced the screen, stood. "Because she had a rash on her hand."

"The rash on her ring finger went away as soon as she started spending quality time with you. Maggie and I both noticed that."

So had Nash, but he was through deluding himself into thinking that Callie cared about him the way he needed her to. Aware the roaring fire had done nothing to dispel the chill in his home, he walked over to the bar and poured them each a neat shot of whiskey.

"She has all these pictures of Seth on her computer." And who could compete with a ghost who, according to everything Nash had heard, had been the most perfect, romantic guy in the entire world?

Hart sipped his drink. "She's making that DVD for Brian. So he'll have something of his dad."

The whiskey burned as it hit Nash's throat, but did nothing to allay the emptiness in his soul. "And one day, when he's older, I am sure that Brian will deeply appreciate everything he discovers about the dad he never got to meet. But right now, he is just a little kid, and he needs more than photos in his life."

Hart took off his jacket then sat down. "Finally, something we can agree upon."

Nash continued to pace. "He needs a man in his life who can give him the love and attention he needs."

"And guess who Brian would like to fill that role?"

Nash looked down at his drink, admitting in weary resignation, "I'd like him to be my son, too. But that's hardly the point."

Hart's eyes were sharp and penetrating. "What *is* the point?"

"Callie is refusing to let us take things any further. Hell, she doesn't even want anyone to know we've been seeing each other." And though he hadn't minded keeping what was happening just between them in the beginning, as time went on, he had started to resent skulking around in the shadows.

"So you're saying she's serious about protecting her reputation?"

Nash finished the rest of his drink and set the glass aside. "I'm saying she's serious about making sure we never get to the point where we actually make a lasting, lifelong commitment to each other."

Hart settled more comfortably on the sofa. "She just wants to see you when it's convenient for her to do so."

"And when it's not, I can damn well find somewhere else to be."

His friend rubbed his jaw. "I can see why you'd be ticked off. No guy ever wants to be treated as a sex object."

Nash rolled his eyes. "It was more than that," he returned impatiently.

"Sure about that?" Hart challenged mildly in return.

Nash thought about the way she had kissed and touched and held him. The way she had looked at him when she thought he wasn't aware. Emotion roiled in his chest. Tightened his throat. "Yes." He moved to the window and focused on the bleak winter weather outside. "She was…"

A heavy silence fell. "What?"

Nash resumed his pacing. "Starting to fall for me, the way I was starting to fall for her."

"And yet—here you are. And there she is."

He pivoted, hurt warring with the anger in his gut. "What are you saying?"

Hart stood and looked him square in the eye. "Just that if you were as giving and patient and understanding as she needs you to be, given what she's been through—and what *you've* been through—you'd probably be spending the Christmas holiday in a whole different way."

CALLIE WAS STILL trying to figure out the best way to make things right when she received a text from Nash at eight that evening. Need to get Brian's presents to you. If he's asleep, can I drop them off now?

Her pulse racing, she texted back, Yes. Now is fine. I'll leave the bunkhouse door open for you. See you soon.

Ten minutes later, his pickup truck cruised down the lane. She was waiting on the front porch of her ranch house, wrapped in her coat and hat, the path to what she hoped would be reconciliation resting in her pocket. Because it was raining again and colder than ever, he parked his pickup so the passenger side aligned with the covered bunkhouse porch. He hopped out and, Stetson slanted rakishly across his brow, opened up the rear passenger door.

Her heart hammering in her chest, she watched as he carried in the toy workshop and two riding tractors he had painstakingly assembled.

Finished, he set the lock and pulled the door shut.

Callie waved him over. He closed up his truck and strode toward her, looking tough and sexy in the evening light. He smelled good, too, like pine and winter and Nash. She tilted her head back, gaze roving his handsome face. Then her throat went tight. "If you have a minute…" she said softly.

The corner of his mouth tipped up beneath the masculine reserve. "I do."

"Good, because I'd really like you to come in."

He followed her into the hall. Waited, more patiently than he ever had.

Callie swallowed hard. "May I take your coat and hat?"

His eyes never leaving hers, he handed them over.

She hung the damp garments on the tree rack. Tried not to throw herself into his arms and beg forgiveness right off the bat. First, she knew, they had a few things to work out.

"Can I offer you some coffee?"

His gaze remained serious, but his smile broadened. "Sounds good," he said huskily.

Nervous now that the moment was upon them, she gestured inanely at the platter of vanilla and chocolate spritz cookies. "There are cookies, too."

He nodded and, ignoring everything else, took her into his arms. His body was warm and strong against hers. He threaded his hands through her hair and gazed down at her. Repentant. Somber. And most of all, gentle. "I'm sorry about the way things ended between us."

She splayed her hands over the steady thrumming of his heart. "So am I. And, just for the record, I don't want what's been between us to end."

"I don't either."

She paused and moved away from him. "But there are some things I have to say before we continue."

He went still. "I'm listening."

"Up until the time my husband died, I led a charmed life. Nothing really bad had ever happened to me, and I had convinced myself it never would. So when I lost Seth so unexpectedly, it turned my whole world upside down. Everything I thought I knew about what the future held was suddenly wrong. And yet I was pregnant, so I knew I had to carry on…"

She released a deep shuddering breath, forced herself to look him in the eye. "So I ignored all the grief and the fear, the pain and the confusion, and I pretended to everyone that I was stronger than anyone had ever expected. Only I wasn't. And I crashed and crashed hard."

He reached over and took her hand, squeezed it encouragingly. With effort, Callie continued, "The medical explanation was a combination of electrolyte imbalance, fatigue and dehydration. A few days of rest and IV fluids, a referral to a grief specialist and a return to my hometown and family, and I was fine again. Or so I thought. Only I wasn't okay, Nash. I haven't been for a long time." She hitched in a breath. "Not until you came along and helped me see that my fear of loss, my refusal to let myself really feel much of anything, was the real enemy."

He took her other hand, too. Studied her kindly. "And you're not afraid anymore?"

She relished the warmth and tenderness of his grip. "I wish I could say I wasn't. I wish I could say that I know I wouldn't crash harder than ever if I lost you, but I can't. What's different now is that I'm willing to forget about holding back. I'm willing to take the risk."

NASH SENSED WHAT it was costing Callie to open up her heart to him like this. But she wasn't the only one who had a confession to make. Hooking his foot beneath a chair, he pulled it away from the table, sank down in it and lowered her onto his lap. Wrapping both arms around her waist, he admitted in a low, rusty-sounding voice, "It's not just you who's been stuck. The truth is—"

and it was a truth she had helped him see "—I've had my guard up for years. Since my brother died, really. Until you and Brian came along, that was. Suddenly, I couldn't turn away."

She offered a tremulous smile.

"Part of it was my attraction to you," he confessed.

She settled more intimately against him, curling one hand around his shoulders, resting the other over his heart. "Our chemistry *is* pretty strong."

He nodded, continuing honestly, "Another part was the way I feel about your son. Because he's not just a cute, engaging, precocious little boy with the biggest heart I've ever seen—" Nash grinned "— he's also so much like you in so many ways it's uncanny."

Callie laughed, admitting, "He does have the McCabe stubbornness and determination."

"Yet another thing I love about him," Nash declared.

Callie sighed contentedly, apparently ready to lighten the mood. "He loves you, too."

But Nash couldn't shift to play until they had worked out their future. In a way that would last this time. More than ready to meet her halfway, he said quietly, "The question is, what do you want from me? Is it friendship? A friends-with-benefits arrangement? A secret love affair? Because whatever it is, Callie," he vowed huskily, "I'm prepared to give it to you." *Because giving is what Christmas is all about.*

She smiled impishly and he felt his mouth curve in return. "How about all of the above, minus the secret component? Plus—" she pulled him closer still, till their lips were just an inch apart "—how about we throw in all the love I have for you—for the rest of my life?"

Love. She'd said she loved him? He kissed her fiercely. "You mean that?"

Nodding, she took his face between her hands. "I do." She kissed him until they were both breathless and then rested her forehead against his. "I love you, Nash."

The softness of her surrender was all he had ever dreamed. "I love you, too." He shifted her off his lap, then stood, as well. "And I'm willing to give you all the time you need. Which is why—" he reached into the pocket of his jeans "—I got you this." He handed her a small velvet box.

Callie opened it up. Inside was the most beautiful garnet he'd been able to find. Judging by the look on her face, it suited her perfectly. "My birthstone," she breathed in delight.

Glad she liked what he'd picked out for her, he said, "To symbolize new beginnings." He took it out of the case, then took her hand in his. "I had the stone mounted on a ring, because the circle—like my love for you— is never ending. And, as you can see," he noted as he carefully slid it over her knuckle, "it goes on your right hand, not your left."

Humor sparkled in her pretty blue eyes as she held out her hand to admire his gift. "Because you're afraid I'll get another rash?"

"No." Shaking his head, he lifted her wrist to his lips. "Because I don't want you wearing a ring on that hand until you're ready."

Color swept into her cheeks. "You do understand."

"I'm sorry I rushed you."

She cuddled against him. "I'm sorry I didn't tell you sooner how I felt." He kissed her again, lingeringly this time.

Finally, she pressed her hand to his chest, drew back reluctantly. With a smile, she admitted, "I got you a present, too."

First was a framed photo of their selfie. "I love it," he said.

"Good, because it's only a hint of all the good times to come."

Second was a card.

"Open it," Callie urged in excitement.

Nash read, "You are cordially invited to spend December 24 and 25 with Callie and Brian at the Heart of Texas Ranch, a place where all your yuletide dreams can come true." He paused to look at her. "You're not going home to Laramie?"

"Not until after Christmas, on the 26th. And when we do, I'd very much like you to accompany us, so I can introduce you properly to my parents and the rest of my sisters."

Nash regarded her solemnly. "You're sure?"

"I am." Callie beamed up at him. "This way we can have the best of both worlds. The new life we're creating, and then the introduction of the rest of the family and friends you'll be joining when you hook up with me."

He flashed her a wicked smile. "Hooking up sounds good," he teased.

"Mommy." A small voice called before he could kiss her again. Familiar footsteps pounded down the stairs. "Santa here?" Brian asked.

"Even better," Callie informed with a smile.

Getting a glimpse of their company, the pajama-clad little boy opened his arms wide. He scampered across the floor. "My friend! Nash!"

"Merry Christmas to you, too, buddy!" Nash said.

Even though the holiday was officially another twenty-eight hours away, it felt as if it was starting now.

"Mer' Chris—" Brian said right back. He hugged Nash and then his mom fiercely before inclining his head toward the exit. "Outside! See, Mommy!"

Perplexed, they headed for the door.

"Well, what do you know!" Callie and Nash stared in disbelief. "Snow?" she breathed.

On December 23! Aware they now had everything they ever wanted and needed, Nash took both Callie and Brian into his arms. "Seems like dreams do come true."

Epilogue

One year later

Callie and Nash were in the ranch house kitchen, assembling a gingerbread house, when the voices drifted out to them from the adjacent playroom.

"I got a daddy," Brian said to his cousin Henry, while the two of them worked on constructing their version of the North Pole with wooden building blocks. "Do you have a daddy?"

"Of course I got a daddy." Henry moved around to put on the roof before adding importantly, "And I got a baby brother, too."

"I'm going to have a baby brother," Brian boasted.

Callie and Nash looked at each other. They had been at this for a month now.

Grinning, Nash rose with gentlemanly leisure. "My turn?"

Contentment flowing through her, Callie smiled back. "Have at it." Because if there was anything she and her new husband had learned, it was that when Brian did not *want* to understand something, he did not *ever* understand something.

"Actually, fellas, Brian might have a baby brother,

and he might have a baby sister," Nash hunkered down to explain to three-and-a-half-year-old Brian and four-year-old Henry. "His mommy and I don't know what kind of baby is in her tummy right now. We're just very happy that she is going to have a baby next summer. It won't matter if it's a girl or a boy."

"I know what it is, Daddy." Disregarding Nash's careful explanation, Brian stood and moved carefully around the beautifully decorated Christmas tree from Echols Mountain to work on the other side of his budding creation. *"It's a boy."*

"Yeah," cousin Henry chimed in, "I think so, too."

Nash stood as well and eyed the gloomy winter weather outside.

Callie knew what her husband was thinking. Rain, not snow, was predicted, but you never knew…especially when they were in the midst of record cold.

Her husband braced his hands on his hips. "Well, like I said, it could be either one, fellas. We'll find out for sure when the baby is born in six months."

"Daddy! We already know," Brian countered in exasperation. "It's a boy. And when he gets here, then we'll have four boys to play with. Me and Henry and his brother and my brother."

Callie strolled in to join them—and rescue Nash. "Seems like you boys have it all figured out."

Brian and Henry scowled. "'Course we do," they said in unison.

Callie took Nash's hand in hers. He squeezed her hand in return. They exchanged smiles and retreated to the adjacent kitchen. It was hard to believe how much her life had changed in just one year, Callie reflected happily, but there was no denying that all was good.

After a six-month courtship that was at once low-key and highly romantic, she and Nash had married at the top of Echols Mountain, with just a few family and friends present. Nash had moved into Callie and Brian's home. And he was using his ranch house as an office to accommodate his growing business.

Once married, they'd gotten busy at expanding their family. And now they were enjoying their second holiday season together. With, she hoped, a very special surprise for them all still to come.

"So what do *you* think?" Nash asked, as Callie spread the creamy white icing over the roof and down the sides of the gingerbread house. "Since you're the one with the miracle growing inside you. Girl or boy?"

"You never know," Callie teased. She dipped an extra piece of gingerbread into the buttercream and lovingly fed it to him. "It could be twins. Possibly even one of each. Multiples do run in my family..."

"Can't say I'd mind that." Nash brought her close and kissed her tenderly on the lips. He tasted of sugar, spice and man. "Although it *would* upset the logistics of Brian and Henry's plans."

Callie shrugged and fed him another piece of icing-dipped cake. "Well, then," she reckoned, "Hart and Maggie would just have to get busy again."

Nash sobered comically and fed her cake, too. "You're right." He dabbed a little bit of icing from the corner of her lip. "Why should we have all the fun?" He threaded his hands through her hair and kissed her again, even more thoroughly this time.

Youthful footsteps pounded on the wood floor behind them. "Ugh! Kissing!" Brian and Henry said in unison.

Reluctantly, Callie and Nash moved apart.

Brian squinted. "Why do grown-ups do that?"

"I don't know," Henry declared, "but my parents are always kissing, too. 'Specially under the mistletoe."

Tired of discussing something he found so disdainful, Brian stepped closer to the kitchen table. "Mommy, is the house ready to decorate?"

Callie brought out the bowls of colorful candy she'd already prepared. "It sure is."

Nash pulled up two chairs. The boys climbed on and got busy. And for a while all was lost in the magic of placing gumdrops and other assorted candies on the yuletide creation.

When they were done, they all stepped back to admire their handiwork Nash looked out the window once again. "Well, what do you know," he said in wonder, shaking his head.

Everyone turned in the direction of his gaze. An older couple was coming up the walk. They looked a little jet-lagged. Their arms were laden with gifts.

Nash turned to Callie, a question in his eyes. "I asked your parents to come," she said softly. "I pointed out that healing the rift would be the best gift of all."

"And they agreed?" he asked hoarsely.

Callie's eyes filled with tears of joy, as she nodded. "They love you, Nash. They always have. They just…" Her voice caught, too. "They had a hard time showing it."

He hugged her close. "This couldn't have been easy," he said in a low, choked voice.

It hadn't been. But there were some things worth fighting for. Family, paramount among them.

She hugged him back, just as ferociously. "They know, with the new baby on the way, it's time we put the heartbreak of the past behind us and start celebrating all that we have now, in this moment. So what do you say?" Callie took Nash's hand and then turned to Brian and his cousin Henry. "Are you fellas ready to greet Nash's mommy and daddy and have them spend Christmas here, too?"

The "fellas" in her life grinned.

"You bet!" they said in unison.

Nash opened the door.

Once again, Callie noted with a smile, they were going to have the Christmas of their dreams.

* * * * *

MILLS & BOON®

Exciting new titles
coming next month

With over 100 new titles available every month,
find out what exciting romances
lie ahead next month.

Visit
www.millsandboon.co.uk/comingsoon
to find out more!